Shadowman

A Novel of Menace

Also by Dennis Etchison

METAHORROR

Shadowman
A Novel of Menace

DENNIS ETCHISON

A DELL BOOK

Published by
Dell Publishing
a division of
Bantam Doubleday Dell Publishing Group, Inc.
666 Fifth Avenue
New York, New York 10103

ISBN: 0-440-21202-2

Printed in the United States of America

TO
HERB YELLIN

Who is the third who walks always
beside you?
When I count, there are only you
and I together
But when I look ahead up the white road
There is always another one walking
beside you. . . .

—T. S. Eliot
The Waste Land

Night falls.

The stars come out.

The moon rises and a horizon line becomes clear, dividing the sky from the world below.

In front of the moon is a hill.

A man is climbing the hill, a silhouette without eyes or features. He moves slowly, bearing a great weight, as though balancing the moon on his shoulders.

When he reaches a gnarled oak tree, he finally releases his grip. A sack sloughs to earth, black and misshapen as a huge lump of coal.

The man picks up a shovel and digs, the long handle sticking out like an extra elbow.

1

He stoops, working lower, piling up a ridge of dirt until the hole is deep enough.

Then he buries his burden.

The horizon is even again, broken only by the outline of the man and the tree. The enormous face of the moon, round and white as a skull, nods in approval.

The man leans on the handle as the moon sinks below the hill. Then he returns his spade to its place beside the tree and begins the long descent to the sleeping valley.

The horizon line fades into blackness.

Now there is nothing but the night.

Part One
The Red Tide

1.

The late-afternoon sun knifed through the windshield. It cut across the surface of the ocean at the end of the street like a blade angled low over the water, slashing rooftops, stabbing the windows of houses and parked cars, impaling everything in its path. Martin's eyes burned. He lowered the visor and leaned back against the headrest, but it was no use. He could not get away.

He put on his dark glasses and climbed out.

In the backseat was a large plastic bag. He dragged it out of the car, slung it over his shoulder and began walking down the street.

The block was lined with small houses set too close together, built years ago in anticipation of a resort boom that never came this far north. The oldest were wood-frame homes with peeling white paint and screened porches. The spaces between were filled by cheap, modern bungalows, a way of squeezing every last dollar from the beachtown lots.

The house she rented was one of these bungalows.

They were difficult to tell apart. He had never been inside, but he remembered the small yard and warped front door from the hours he had spent staking it out shortly after she left him. Late one day he saw her pull into the driveway. *You're not Leanne,* Martin said as he came up next to it, and immediately felt like a fool. The man behind the wheel glanced at him with mild irritation, as if confronted by a panhandler. *You must be Jack,* lifting a take-out bag from the seat beside him. *Excuse me, Jack, but I have to get this inside—Lee doesn't like cold pasta.* Then he noticed the prosthetic hook in place of one hand and, instead of reaching in and bashing the man's head against the steering wheel, Martin muttered something apologetic and withdrew. He spent the night on Will's couch in Eden Cove and did not try again.

I should have done it, he thought now. Hauled him out by the short hairs and bloodied his nose right here in front of her house. Lee, my ass. What does he know about my wife?

The trouble was, she probably would have sided with her lover if she found him lying there on the ground, that smirk smeared across his face. She always sided with the underdog. As long as she wasn't married to him.

He recognized the leaded-glass rainbow in the window and the barbecue grill on the porch. He had purchased both for another house. They were here now, relics from some other time and place. At first he was confused by the initials on the mailbox. Then he remembered her maiden name.

The bag grew heavy.

Leave it on the porch, he told himself, just drop it off and get away, the way you planned it.

Instead he walked on by.

At the end of the block he stopped. Ahead lay the bike path and the guardrail above the grassy dunes. The sun was cooling, turning coral behind a layer of industrial haze from the south. There was no one left out on the sand, not even children. It was that time of day when people leave beaches everywhere, feeling vaguely melancholy, wondering what they had come for and whether they would ever find it. Martin gazed back into the dying eye of the sun and did not blink.

He left the cliff and walked back up the empty street.

This time he unlatched the gate and approached the door. There was no car in the driveway yet; he was thankful for that much. He avoided looking through the windowpane. He knew he would see the furniture he had ordered in a last attempt to please her the day before she moved out. It hadn't worked, but she had taken the sofa and chairs with her anyway.

He dropped the bag on the doormat.

It sighed as the air went out of it and the black plastic deflated around the lumpy contents. In the bag were things that had slipped down in the back of the closet and been forgotten. There were not that many items, but it had taken him all day to get them together. She had never called or returned to collect any of it. He did not know if she cared or even remembered what she had left behind, but he could wait no longer.

It ends here, he thought.

He took an envelope out of his pocket. On it he had written:

Lee—

    Here is the extra key to the house. I have cleaned out my things. The broker can put it up for sale as soon as you sign the papers.

    I'm staying at Will's if you need to get in touch with me.

J.

He read the note again. Now the words seemed all wrong. He couldn't leave it here; he did not want the man with the hook to find it first. It was a mistake. But it was too late to change. He should have written the message on a separate slip of paper and sealed it inside with the key. If he got rid of the envelope and left only the key on top of the bag, would she see it? If she did, would she understand?

He stuffed the envelope back into his pocket. Then he picked up the bag, slung it over his shoulder again, and turned away from the door.

At the end of the block a boy on a bicycle glanced up, saw him coming this way and pedaled rapidly past the intersection without looking back.

I must look like hell, Martin thought. Like some kind of evil Santa Claus with a black bag on my back.

Well, it's not my choice. I didn't want it this way.

He crossed the bikepath and descended the cliffs to the beach. When the stairs stopped he dug in his heels and slid on down the dunes. The sand sucked at his feet but did not slow him. He walked out to the sea.

A breeze whipped along the shore, spattering him with sharp, wet grains of sand. He ignored this. He lowered his head, swung the bag like a hammer and let go. It flew out of his hands and landed at the edge of the water. Foamy waves lapped the plastic, tipped the bag over and began to carry it away.

He sniffed the air and wrinkled his nose. There would be a red tide tonight. Already the stench was here, a mix of dead fish and plankton and the bacteria that would eventually devour it all.

The sooner the better, he thought.

He headed back through the tall grass and climbed the dunes.

At the guardrail, he looked down one last time.

There was the bag, bobbing on the water like a fat man. But now the tide was rising. Instead of drifting out to sea the bag floated languidly back to shore. As he watched, it caught on a mass of beached kelp and did not move again. He waited for the tide to claim it, but there it remained.

He thought, I can't even do this much right.

He fumbled in his pocket for the envelope, which he tore open and discarded. Then he took the key, held it high, cocked his arm and hurled it at the setting sun.

The silver key arced through the air and dropped short, falling into the seaweed.

The bag flopped forward as if nodding, mocking him.

He ran back across the sand, reached down into the kelp and ripped at the plastic. The neatly arranged contents tumbled out: a blouse, a skirt, a camisole, a pair of sandals, entwined belts, a scarf, various unmatched socks, a flannel nightgown, panties, a stack of magazines, old jeans and more, even the set of watercolor paints he had given her last Christmas, never used.

Cursing, he clawed at her things and tossed them furiously into the water. The heavier clothing and magazines withered and sank, but some of the undergarments continued to float like lilies. Finally there was only the plastic garbage bag. He threw

11

it, too. It flapped away on the breeze like a bird with torn wings.

He stood there panting with rage, his heart hammering, the sweat chilling his skin.

At last it was done.

Almost.

One more garment was left: a T-shirt, still caught in the glistening kelp. He gave it a pull but it did not come loose. He yanked harder. To his surprise, it shredded in his fingers.

He stared at it, trying to understand.

The fabric was covered with slime and already rotting. As he held it, a miniature crab scuttled out of a hole in the material, spidered over his thumb, and plopped to the sand.

He squinted and knelt down.

There was something else caught in the olive-drab seaweed. What appeared to be the remains of—but it wasn't possible.

He could not believe his eyes.

It was the body of a child.

She lay there tangled in the fronds, face pale and swollen, the lips and ears and some other parts blue-black, the stomach puffed out like a starving African's, the tiny ribs showing white as knuckles under the stretched and bloated skin. The legs and lower portions were missing. Horrified, Martin smoothed the hair away from the cold face. Some of the strands came loose in his fingers. He shook them off his hand as a chill ran up his arm to his chest. It opened a hollow place behind his rib cage and spread along his other arm and down his legs to his toes, then crept back up, going for his throat. He could no longer feel his lips but knew they must be moving. He heard only the surf that boomed through the earth and roared in his ears.

He stumbled away toward the cliffs.

On the other side of the guardrail, halfway up the short street, a pale yellow light winked on in Leanne's front window.

Already it was coming on cold, sooner than she expected.

She killed the ignition and sat in the car a moment longer, rubbing her arms as the heater shut down. She was bone-tired. There was a moist rasping in her lungs when she breathed; it reminded her of wet wings scraping the inside of her chest. And her breasts ached. All day she had wanted to unhook her bra to relieve the pressure, but now the ache was deeper, as if something were eating away at her heart.

Shivering, she got out of the car and carried the bag of groceries to the porch. She had a strong feeling that she was forgetting something. What was missing? Standing in the driveway, she tried to remember.

The wind whipped in her ears. She heard the rising and falling surf, a car accelerating in the distance, the ringing of a telephone that no one cared to answer. Nothing else. Nothing at all.

Then it came to her.

Every day for most of the year that she had lived here, there were always children playing, chasing each other up and down the stairs to the beach, the gliding arc of their Frisbees like descending UFO's against the sunset. Once she had come home to find a little boy climbing up the side of her house to retrieve a toy airplane that had landed on her roof. Where was he—where were they all —now? The last few months she had barely registered their high voices and the moving blur of their faces between the houses, so that their presence was something to be taken for granted . . . until today. When had they gone away? Last week? Last month? She hadn't noticed. Perhaps they had found a better place to play. In any event, it didn't have anything to do with her.

And what was that smell? It was blowing in on the sea breeze. At the end of the block a small square of beach showed beyond the rail. The sky above was streaked with fading colors, the surface of the sea black as an oil slick. She unlocked the door and ducked inside, not wanting to know.

As she turned on the light and set the groceries down, the phone rang.

She waited for the answering machine to take over.

A beep.

Then, "Lee?"

She listened impassively to the voice from the machine's speaker.

"Lee, it's Steve . . ."

She didn't feel well enough to talk to him. She hadn't felt truly well since marrying Jack and moving to this town six years ago. It was like a lingering disease that she could not shake. Her health wouldn't be right again till she could get away. Far away.

"Lee, please pick up. I know you're there. . . ."

"Thanks for calling," said the voice chip in

her machine as his thirty seconds ended, and hung up.

She turned it off. I'll talk to him later, she thought. When he calls back. He always does.

She closed the curtains and sat down in her cane rocker.

It was as if she had been holding her breath all afternoon, waiting for this time alone. Now her chest wheezed worse than ever, tightening painfully. She inhaled deeply to clear her passages, but that hurt even more.

She lit a menthol cigarette, blew out a long cone of smoke, and fell into a coughing fit. When she got up she was dizzy. She passed through the bedroom and held her head down over the bathroom sink, hacking and spitting as she regained her balance. Outside a wave drummed the shore, resonating through the shaky foundation, and a car slowed in the alley behind her house. Still nauseous, she opened her eyes.

She saw an unfamiliar face in the mirror.

The eyes were not hers, they couldn't be. Those bags! And the skin, the blotches . . .

I look like hammered shit, she thought.

She examined her profile, pressing her hands against her stomach. Fat! She lifted up her sweater. Her breasts were too large. She wished she could cut them off. Disgusted, she leaned close to the mirror.

Was that a pimple? At her age? She leaned closer, almost touching the glass, and squeezed the spot on her forehead with her fingernails. Two half-moon crescents cut into her skin and she began to bleed.

She found astringent in the medicine cabinet, moistened a cotton ball. The mark on her forehead was enlarged, hideous. How could she go to work tomorrow looking like this? She slammed the medicine cabinet too hard. The dry-rotted wood that framed the mirror started to splinter and break loose . . .

She froze as she saw what was about to happen. The bottom of the frame falling into the sink. The mirror hesitating before dropping straight down as if in slow motion and fracturing into sharp pieces. A long shard of glass flipping over the edge of the basin and hitting the floor an inch from her foot, sticking upright like a jackknife. Her legs stepping back and meeting the side of the tub, her arms splaying hopelessly as she lost control. Clutching desperately, her fingers somehow finding the shower curtain. The plastic tearing loose. Struggling to stay upright in

17

the tub, her head striking the tiles, and then the blood . . .

The phone rang again.

She blinked.

The mirror was still intact.

She held the doorjamb for support, then passed back through the bedroom to the living room and unplugged the phone cord from the wall.

In the kitchen, she poured a shot of tequila out of the good bottle Jack had brought from Mexico and forced herself to take a sip. It was smooth at first, like a liqueur, then burned going down. Maybe it would clear her head. She refilled the shot glass to the brim and started back to the living room.

As the front door rattled.

She stiffened at the sound.

A wave boomed, vibrating the window.

It was only the tide, coming in or going out, she didn't know which.

She relaxed and went to her chair.

The door rattled again, more forcefully this time, as if something had brushed against it.

Was it the cat, the stray? She had fed it so often that it thought it belonged to her. She couldn't leave it outside . . .

She stood up too fast. The blood rushed from her head and the tequila spilled.

At that instant there was a loud noise in the kitchen, and the back door popped open.

"Lee?" said a man's voice.

He came into the living room, smirking. One hand supporting a pizza carton.

"Steve, what are you doing here?"

"I brought din-din," he said. "Hungry?"

"No." She realized that she still held the shot glass and put it down, wiping her hand on her sweater. "I thought you were going to call first."

"I did. But you weren't answering." He set the carton on the table, revealing what should have been his hand. He brandished the hook like a pointer. "Do we have any wine left?"

"Steven—"

"You don't look so good." He crossed the room and tried to kiss her.

She turned her face away.

"What's the matter?"

"I think I'm coming down with something," she said.

He sauntered toward the bedroom, picking at his necktie with his metal pincer. He kicked off his shoes.

"What a week," he said.

19

"Steven, I'm awfully tired. I don't know if this is such a good idea."

"Go ahead and start," he called, "while it's hot." He pulled out the sweatpants and shirt he kept in the closet. "Then I'll tell you all about my day."

She heard the bedsprings creak as he sat on the edge of the mattress.

There was a half-inch of tequila in the bottom of the glass. She tossed it back and opened the carton. The pizza was a mass of hardening cheese with red spots showing through. Some of it stuck to the lid, like the strands of an afterbirth. She put a hand over her mouth to keep from gagging.

Now the rattling sound came again from the front door.

It was definitely a knock.

"Steven, please . . . can you get that?"

No answer from the bedroom.

She pulled herself together, went reluctantly to the door, and drew the curtain away from the upper pane.

Only darkness outside.

She took hold of the knob. Before she could twist it, the latch gave way in the warped frame and the door swung open.

A man was standing in shadow on the porch, his fist raised to knock again. His bright blue eyes were round and wide in a face swimming with perspiration.

"Jack?"

Then she noticed that the whites of his eyes were pink, and that the wetness on his cheeks was more than sweat.

"Sorry, Lee," he said with great difficulty, "but . . ."

She started to reach out to steady him, thought better of it. "What's wrong?"

"Call the police," he said.

"Are you serious?"

She stood aside as he staggered into the house. He looked terrible. He had sand on his trousers and beach tar on his hands and his face was unnaturally white under a salty film.

"Just do it," he said.

She plugged in the phone with shaking hands. "All right, I'm calling. Sit before you fall down. Did something happen? Is that it?"

An officer came on the line. She reeled off her name and address. Then she put her palm over the mouthpiece.

"They want to know what this is regarding. What should I tell them?"

Martin shambled across the living room, ready to collapse.

21

There was the sound of the toilet flushing. Steven came out of the bedroom, drawing his sweatshirt over his belly. The pincer clicked nervously and lost its hold on the bottom of the shirt. She was shocked at how fat he had let himself get. She wanted to pull the shirt down for him, but the officer on the line was losing patience.

"Tell them there's a body on the beach," Martin said.

"A *what*?"

"What the hell is *he* doing here?" said Steven.

She held the receiver close to her mouth and repeated what Martin had said, speaking rapidly, as if it were important to get it out while she still had the chance.

"Sorry," Martin muttered. "The phone. I needed . . ."

"You're God damned right you're sorry," said the other man. "You're one sorry bastard, let me tell you."

She hung up quickly. "Steven—"

"Look at him. He looks like a bum."

"Steven!"

"Don't you ever shave?" he said to Martin. "Don't you have a job? What are you, one of those homeless sons of bitches?"

Martin turned around uncertainly, his

shoulders hunched, took a faltering step toward the sofa and began to lower himself gingerly down onto the cushions, as carefully as an old man.

"Oh, no you don't!"

"Steven, come with me." She attempted to steer him away. "I want to talk to you."

"Look at his clothes . . . !"

She led him to the kitchen. His face was livid, the vein standing out at his temple. She felt his arm trembling.

"It's all right," she said. "I let him in."

"I don't want him in this house!"

She saw the way his lips curled back from his teeth, the naked fury. Now his face was compressed, ugly. He's losing his hair, she thought, staring at his bulging forehead. I never noticed.

"Calm down," she said.

"He's in there ruining my sofa!"

"*Your* sofa?" She made a decision. "I think you'd better go home now."

"You want *me* to leave?"

"I don't like this macho bullshit. You're behaving like a little boy."

"Then tell him to get out." Flecks of spittle shone like whiteflies in the air in front of his mouth. "Or I will. I'll break his fucking—"

"Fine," she said, grabbing her keys. "You

23

two can slug it out. All I know is, I don't need it."

She started out of the kitchen.

The sofa was empty. Martin was no longer in the living room. The door stood open. Now a light blipped round and round outside, staining her house crimson.

She saw Martin seated in the back of a squad car. At the end of the short street, past the guardrail, other police officers disappeared over the edge of the dune cliff, their flashlights piercing the darkness like swords.

Steven came up behind her.

"Thank God," he said. "They got him."

"What are you talking about? They're not here to arrest him! They're here because of the body." It's happened again, she thought.

She realized what had happened to all the children. They don't play outside now because their parents won't let them. It's too dangerous.

He wormed his hand and his hook around her waist and up under her arms. "What body?"

Somehow she knew it was a child this time, too.

"Leave me alone," she said.

"I was only trying to protect you, Lee."

"From *what*?"

24

"Can't you see? He's obviously unstable . . ."

Incredibly, she felt his hook sliding under her sweater and then the cold steel picking at her bra, mechanically drubbing her nipple through the stitched cloth. She took hold of his wrist where metal joined flesh.

"What, exactly," she hissed, "do you think you're doing?"

2.

Shadow Bay is shrouded in fog for six months out of every year. As the days grow short a gray blanket creeps in from the coast, clouding the houses at the base of the foothills, collecting around the barren trees until they resemble giant mushrooms. The town becomes a place of dampness and rust, of barking dogs that are seldom seen, of creaking signs and pale traces of neon, of power lines that crackle through the night as if underwater; of knuckles swelling slowly numb, of looming shapes and distant traffic and the cries of gulls far behind you and in front of you all at once; of a numinous moon drifting like a gauze-covered face. There is dripping condensation from broken drain-pipes, the clutching of wild wings in moldering garages, salt glaze on glass, mildewed gloves and too-thin socks, soft newspapers and food that is never hot, litter dropped in gutters melting into paste, laundry wilting before it can be put away, labels buckling from jars in musty cupboards, white breath frosting windows like steam from the tidepools on the beaches down below. Children wait indoors for the season to end, until it is so late in the year that it ceases to matter. Sickly faces stare blankly in classrooms, pallid fingers lie thickly on desks, eyes turn milky and begin to shine with a different, more fearful light.

In this town there were four boys who could not wait.

Robby, Kevin, Jamie and David took the long way home from school every day, making plans to find each other again after dark despite their parents' new rules, to slip out when they were supposed to be studying and walk the back streets, exploring the limits of their world. The oldest was David, almost thirteen. On these walks he listened to their complaints with the patience of a natural leader, and offered quiet advice to help them through the unbearably long winter.

Until they noticed that someone was following them.

It was only another boy, a little boy, much younger than they were. His name was Christopher and he was eight years old; at least that was what he said. That was too young, of course. But they could not lose him, so David finally gave him permission to tag along. . . .

They continued in this way, five of them now, walking and talking till there was nothing left to say, till the town and everyone in it was theirs for the knowing, or so it seemed.

And then one night when the air was sharp and the moon broke through to show the way, David led them beyond the city limits to the edge of the redwoods on the inland side of the basin, where the hills formed a natural ridge around the bay, holding their town separate and isolated from the great world beyond.

That was the night they went all the way into the forest.

They made their way up a steep path to the top of the hills, slipping back two steps for every three they took. Their socks sagged, scooping dank sand, the path collapsing beneath them in a whispering succession of footholds, so that by the time they came to the place where the wildwoods began, Christopher felt that he was lost in a nightmare of endless climbing.

When they reached level ground he lagged back, trying to ignore the sound of twigs breaking underfoot, of the sticky leaves that settled behind him like ghostly rain.

"Here?"

"Not yet," David told him.

"Why did he have to come?" said Jamie.

"He's only a kid," said Kevin.

"It's past his bedtime," said Robby.

Christopher sat down on the ground. He heard the others kicking tree trunks, knocking the dirt out of their treads. He was cold and tired but he was not going to admit it. He hugged his sides and did not say anything more.

A long minute passed as the boys recovered, picking grit from their eyes. The night pressed in around them with an almost palpable presence. Christopher waited for David to take out his flashlight and lead them the rest of the way. Someone cracked his knuckles. Then there was only the sound of their breathing, and the pounding of the faraway surf as it rushed up through the earth to lodge in their chests, locking tight with the rhythm of their hearts.

Ahead was the last plateau, framed by a gnarled, misshapen bower of old branches. As Christopher stared into it, straining to penetrate the darkness, the passage seemed to deepen till it became the yawning mouth of a tunnel beckoning them still deeper into the high country.

"Let's go," said David.

The boys converged in loose single file beneath the arms of the trees. A faint crumpling resumed under their feet, a wet bending and the pattering of droplets as fog clung to split wood, trickled over slippery bark and fell into the muddied leaves and shoots at their ankles. The passage went on and on. When they finally came through to the other side, to the edge of a bare, skeletal glade, Christopher forced himself to keep up. He was not sure he wanted to be here, after all, but that was something he could never let them know.

David surveyed the clearing. In the center was a firepit rimmed by stones. His eyes fixed past it, to the far embankment leading up to the plateau.

"Wait here," he said.

He left them there and went across the

clearing alone. When he reached the embankment he paused. Then he climbed up to the top and was gone.

"Where did he go?" said Kevin.

"He'll be back," said Jamie.

"He wouldn't just leave us," said Robby.

A sound came from the bushes at their backs.

"What's that?"

It was only a bullfrog, but at the same instant a cricket chimed in with its sawing chirrup, the two sounds synching in an eerie cacophony: close, closer and then gradually receding like an unexpected wind on its way to the sea.

Now a disembodied arm appeared out of the mist, waving them on.

"All clear," said Jamie.

"Is that him?"

"Well, who do you think?"

The boys followed Jamie, staying close together. In the middle of the clearing they picked up the pace and clambered ahead, eager to get across.

"Chris?" said a voice. It sounded like David's. "Chris, over here . . ."

Christopher ran the rest of the way. He climbed the embankment, anchoring his fingers between the stones and pulling himself up.

David was waiting on the overhang. Christopher took his hand and was yanked the last few feet with such force that he almost went over the edge.

"Take a look at this," said David.

Christopher huffed on his hands, then let out a gasp.

David was already climbing down to join the others. He was alone.

He looked again, and could hardly believe what he saw. Spread before him, all the way from the precipice to the tops of the hills on the far side of town, was a fleecy, undulating carpet. At this altitude the winds had stratified the layers of fog into a vast horizontal plain that reached from the cliffs to the farthest corners of the coastal basin, a wide and opalescent stage bathed in an unearthly glow.

When Christopher opened his mouth again, nothing came out.

The world as he had known it lay far below, buried and all but invisible, like the rapidly dissolving membrane of a dream.

On the oceanward side, at the outermost edge of the cloud cover, the highway was washed out under a reflective haze, a chain of automobile headlights no brighter than a necklace of dusty jewels. The swishing of tires blended with the easy cadence of the tide sliding into shore, while high above the water, serene and unmoving, the chipped, phosphorescent eye of the moon hung behind a solitary white strand, its radiance transfusing the valley into a billowing, iridescent vision.

"Is this it?"

"Aw, I was here before . . ."

"Who's got the matches?"

The voices of Robby, Kevin and Jamie, so far away.

Christopher let the hairs settle into place on the back of his neck. He hunkered there. He hid his face and cried softly and did not know why.

Below him, the other boys were building a fire.

After a long time he went down to join them.

The fire was low. David stirred the damp wood with a pepper branch and sat staring into the dying flames. The embers loosed the last of their sparks in a weak updraft and settled again, a sizzle of sodden eucalyptus pods. A sweet rank smoke blew into Christopher's face and made him cough.

"It's getting late, guys," David told them.

"What do you mean?" said Kevin.

He whispered something in Robby's ear. Then Robby leaned over and passed it on to Jamie.

Jamie nodded and pointed at Christopher.

"It's because of *him*. He has to go home, doesn't he?"

"He doesn't have a home," said Kevin.

"He forgot to tell his mother," said Robby.

"He doesn't *have* a mother," said Kevin.

"Then," said Jamie, "if something happened to him, nobody would ever know, would they?"

"Leave him alone," said David.

Christopher looked over their heads to the tangled path along which they had come, to the weathered rocks and the trees and the bowl of the sky above them, above the faces that were bleached by the light of the silently wheeling stars. He had heard what they said but he didn't care. Everything was different now; nothing would ever be the same again. The other boys didn't understand. They hadn't seen. Even if they had, would it make any difference?

A high breeze gusted nearby, catching in a hollow and keening like a human voice.

"Anybody know any stories?" said Kevin.

He had a half-smile on his face. That meant it wasn't a real question. The way he said it, Christopher could tell that Kevin already knew the answer.

"Yeah," said Robby, "a real *good* story!"

Robby and Kevin looked at Jamie, waiting for him to say it.

"I know one," Jamie said.

Then they looked at David.

But David was barely listening. He stood up, stuck his hands in the back pockets of his jeans, and stepped onto a boulder that was worn shiny as a bald head. He peered through an opening in the rock embankment. Beyond the precipice, the cloud cover was breaking up into buttermilk clumps. Soon the insect eyes of the city streets would be visible again.

"Okay?" said Jamie.

David shrugged. "Chris?"

Christopher nodded bravely.

"Okay," said David. "Let's hear your story."

The boys moved closer to the fire.

36

The sounds of the ocean, the muffled traffic, the rustling of the silver-tipped leaves faded away.

Jamie closed his eyes and began to speak, slowly at first, then more forcefully as the words took on a life of their own.

Here is the story he told:

THE LOST PLATOON

This is a true story. It happened a long time ago, when there was a war . . .

One day the fighting got too close to home.

The Captain said, Men, we have to hold the city. We only have one company left. We need reinforcements.

One of the men said, Captain, I'll go.

But the Captain said, No, you might not make it, and then what would happen to the rest of us? We'd still be waiting here when they break through and kill every last man.

So someone else said, Captain, send two of us. That way we can split up and one will get through for sure.

But the Captain said, No way. What if they capture you both? Then where would we be? Even worse off than we are now.

So another one said, Captain, send three of us, sir. And another one and another one said the same thing, Send four or five or six of us, sir, please. It's better than staying here.

But the Captain said, Listen up. If I send the whole company, who'll be here to hold the city? We can't just leave. I have a wife and baby down there, and by God those bastards are not going to get them.

Besides, an army travels on its stomach, and we're running out of supplies. If we lay low we won't use up so many calories and we'll last a lot longer.

I know what, said the First Lieutenant. We have two platoons in this company, right? I'll lead one platoon to find help. We'll move fast, after it gets dark, and stay awake all night and shoot anything that moves. The other platoon can stay here in that big cave on top of the mountain. You keep the food and water. We'll take the canteens off the bodies we kill. I know for a fact that a soldier can live for three-and-a-half weeks on nothing but water. Meanwhile, you listen for the enemy. If they get here first, well, you'll just have to hold them off with everything you've got.

That's a very military idea, said the Captain. He was thinking about the cave. There might be bats or poisonous snakes in it, but that would just have to be tough shit. If there was one thing he knew, it was that war is hell.

When the war is over, Lieutenant, the Captain said, you will get a medal for this. I'll see to it personally.

If your plan works.

And he looked hard at the young Lieutenant like he was his own son.

The Captain ordered his men to seal up the cave with dynamite and leave a hole for air and rifle barrels. That way they would be safe from a surprise attack, and the enemy wouldn't know they were there till the Captain saw the whites of their eyes.

The Lieutenant made a blood oath that the first thing he would do when he got back with the reinforcements would be to blow the cave open again and let them out.

Then he took his platoon and left.

The days turned into weeks. The Captain kept track by cutting marks on the wall with his bayonet.

He told the men not to worry because he trusted the Lieutenant as if he was his own son.

It got later and later in the year . . .

One day the men were too weak to stand up. They ate the last of their C-rations and took turns lying down under the hole in the rocks so they could breathe.

A Private First Class said, Sir, the men can't take it anymore.

It won't be much longer, the Captain told him. Help is on the way. It will be here soon.

But what if they didn't make it? said the Private First Class. What if something happened to them? What if they forgot about us?

The Captain couldn't believe the Lieutenant wouldn't keep his blood oath no matter what. But he asked his platoon what they thought.

They could hardly talk, but they all said the same thing as the Private First Class.

So the Captain had to do something.

He couldn't let his men outside. The enemy might be sneaking up on them, and then they'd be tortured in a way that was worse than death. Besides, they didn't have any dynamite left and they didn't have enough strength to dig out, anyway.

The Captain stood up.

He told them that his plan was this: he was going to explore the rest of the cave. Maybe it went all the way through the mountain and came out on the other side, where the city was. If it did, he could warn the people to evacuate before the enemy got there. Then he would come back and lead his platoon to food and water.

The men shook hands with their Captain. One of them gave him the last piece of beef jerky. Another one gave him a letter, in case anything happened. Another one gave him his Zippo lighter so he could find the way. Nobody showed any emotion. They just stood at attention. They had to hold onto each other to keep from falling down. Then they saluted him and sang "The Stars and Stripes Forever."

The last time they saw the Captain, he was waving from far away down the tunnel. After a while they couldn't see him anymore.

They sat down and waited. Most of them went right to sleep. The Private First Class stood guard.

It was the longest night of their lives. They lost track of time. Their tongues swelled up like pieces of meat. Then they started to go crazy. Crazy with hunger.

They were sure they were doomed. Even the Captain had abandoned them.

One of the men died of starvation. The others dogpiled on top of him and tore his clothes off, which were nothing but rags.

And then you know what they did?

They built a fire and threw him in.

When the body was half-cooked, they picked his skeleton clean like soldier ants. They sucked every last drop of blood. They didn't know what they were doing. They only knew they wanted to live.

That satisfied them for a little while. But the one who died was very skinny. They were already getting hungry again.

They looked at each other to see who would be next.

But no one else died. Their instinct to live was too strong.

So they decided to draw straws.

Then the Private First Class stepped up and said, Men, I'm making the supreme sacrifice. I'm going to lay down my life so that others can live.

And he stabbed himself right there in front of them.

This time they didn't bother with the fire. They just tore him apart like animals. They went ahead and ripped pieces off and stuffed them in their mouths. . . .

They heard a sound.

Something was coming towards them. Something huge and black, with scales all over its body. Its arms were sticking straight out. Its eyes were burning like flashlights. It wasn't moving very fast, but they could tell that nothing could stop it.

The men were paralyzed with fear. Some of them still had fat and blood and pieces of guts dripping out of their mouths.

It came closer and closer to the fire . . . and they saw what it was.

The Captain!

He was walking real slow because there were snakes wrapped around his legs! It was his shadow on the cave wall that made him look so tall. His eyes were glowing because of the fire. And the scales were bats—thousands and thousands of bats, hanging from his arms!

The men backed away.

Do not be afraid, said the Captain. His voice was strange. He said, I tried to find the way. But the passage was blocked. There is no way out.

The Captain had been lost for weeks. Finally he tripped over a nest of snakes, and they bit him so many times that his body went into a state of shock. His bloodstream turned to pure venom. After that he was changed. He could think of only one thing:

To kill.

I have come back for you as I promised, he said.

He was completely insane by now. But he remembered the young Lieutenant, the one he had trusted

41

like his own son, the one who had broken his blood oath.

Come, said the Captain, and follow me.

And they followed.

He started clawing at the rocks and boulders with his bare hands . . .

It took years for them to dig out. Their fingers and hands wore off till they only had bloody stumps, but they kept on digging.

When they finally broke through, it was night outside.

The city and everyone in it was destroyed. The war was over.

But not for them.

The Captain said, Men, this will be your last mission.

Go and find the ones who betrayed us. Do not rest until you have hunted them down. Every one except the Lieutenant, for he is mine.

So they went forth to seek revenge.

They're still out there. They walk by night. They come out of their cave after dark, searching for the cowards who left them there to die. When they find them they will eat them alive.

Sometimes you can see them in the moonlight. They are shadow men. Their faces are like skulls and their uniforms are rotting and falling apart and the bones are sticking out through their skin. You can't stop them. Nothing ever stopped them and nothing ever will stop them . . .

Because they are the Lost Platoon.

Jamie's voice stopped.

There was a tense silence. The boys had drawn nearer the smoldering fire, holding their knees, the soles of their tennis shoes fanned out like a circle of dirty hands around the coals. Now muscles eased, necks bent, chests relaxed, breaths were released.

They looked around as if waking up.

The stark terrain pressed closer to the campsite, more oppressive than ever. The sky had closed above them; an impenetrable darkness hung over the camp, and the sounds they heard, like the shifting of an enormous unseen presence, might have been the brushing of unspeakable wings against the dark side of the moon.

"That was good," said Kevin.

"Yeah," said Robby, "*real* good."

David stood up. "Where's Chris?"

Jamie laughed.

A wind circled the campsite, shaking the trees. Branches parted and more stars shone through, as clear and cold and unblinking as eyes.

"Did anybody see where he went?"

"Not me."

"Not me."

"Maybe he peed his pants," said Jamie, and laughed again.

"Is that all you wanted?" David asked. "To scare him?"

"Well . . . it was a good story, wasn't it?"

"Yeah. A good story."

43

There was a new sound. This time it wasn't the wind. It wasn't like the wind at all.

David grabbed his flashlight and stepped across the firepit, sending ashes spiraling up like fireflies.

"Come on," he said. "We better find him— *fast.*"

Somewhere nearby, a bird screeched.

Christopher zipped up his pants and backed away from the oak tree.

There was a pressure at his back, daring him to turn around. He heard or thought he heard the bowing of misty branches, the oozing of sap from polished leaves and a slow uncoiling within the burrows of the soil.

These things did not frighten him.

I know why they told that story, he thought. It was because of me. They think I'm a baby. But I'm not. Not anymore.

If he got back before it was over, nobody would even know he had been gone.

He turned, trying to remember the way. The moon was hiding now and the stars were too far away. Where was the fire? He turned, turned again.

44

There was the fallen tree. That meant the clearing was this way. Yes, he was sure.

He saw open ground ahead and started off.

"Chris . . . ?" someone called.

He heard the unmistakable sound of footsteps in the mulch.

They're looking for me, he thought. But I'll get back to the camp before they do. I'll laugh at them.

"Chris, where are you?"

The sound of breaking wood was all around him.

He jumped over the gutted tree trunk, caught his toe, lost his balance and began to fall. His hands came down on something soft. Something cold.

The beam of a flashlight jiggled toward him.

"Chris, is that you?"

David shone the beam at the muddy ground.

"Over here!" he shouted.

Then the others were there, crowding next to David, pointing down.

Christopher saw what he had tripped over.

It was part of a large doll. All that was left was the legs. They were torn off, as though the body had been ripped in half by animals. What was there was badly decomposed. As

Chris pulled his hands free some of the flesh came away from the thighbone like boiled meat. Then he got a whiff of it, and he knew that it was not a doll.

"Holy shit," said Kevin.

"Is that what I think it is?" said Jamie.

"Gross," said Robby.

"Chris, wait . . . !" called David.

But too late.

Christopher was running as fast as he could toward the path, wet leaves skidding off his face and head, his breath ragged in his ears.

He wasn't afraid of the night. He wasn't afraid of the forest. He wasn't afraid of the boys and their silly story.

He was afraid of something else, something barely remembered, something that did not have a name.

3.

They asked a lot of questions, but there was nothing Martin could tell them that would make any difference. For now he tried to think only of the sequence that would get him away from the police station as quickly as possible.

He inserted his key with shaking hands. The buzzer sounded. He closed the car door. The buzzer stayed on. He concentrated, opened the door and slammed it again. Then he drew the seat belt across his chest. The buzzer shut off. That was it. *Of course.* He twisted the key. The engine started.

He gripped the wheel and bore down.

Some of the fog was locked inside with him. It etched pictures on the glass. He turned on the defroster. The pictures faded, but every time he released another breath the streaks reappeared, pulsing in and out like a ghostly movie projected on the windshield. The forms shifted against the passing lights, frosty pale and then dark and wet, as if breathing with him.

He focused past the pictures and kept moving.

Shadow Bay was closing down early. A few members of the homeless population were now ambulating in and out of alleys and covered doorways. He drove by a small grocery, an art gallery, a silversmith's, an antique store, a potter's. Only the self-serve gas station and a diner had left their signs on. Dusty terra-cotta lips opened wide in the potter's window, while in the antique dealer's ancient furniture with frayed fabric and cracked leather withdrew into the shadows, out of the reach of his headlights. He did not look too closely at the displays as he passed.

The road split at the end of the main street, one fork leading to the waterfront where he had started a few hours ago, the other inland toward the ridge of foothills behind the bay. He was so tired that he took the wrong turn. After a while he passed a dense residential development where families were settling in for the night before flickering television sets.

48

As soon as he saw the dirt road to the abandoned landfill, he turned around and sped back in the other direction, out of town and up the dark coast.

The moon skimmed along the water beyond the cliffs, keeping pace with his car. He pushed the speed but could not shake it. The dashboard instruments bathed him in a soft glow; he shivered despite the warmth from the heater. When he flexed his hands in the cool light he discovered that his fingers were without feeling, cold and growing colder with each mile.

A few minutes outside of town, something darted across the road.

He hit the brakes.

A pair of mirrored eyes turned to meet him, locked in the glare of his headlights, and froze.

He pumped the pedal harder, heard a thud, and glanced in the rearview mirror.

He saw the fog, tinted red by his taillights. Nothing else.

He made a U-turn, backed onto the shoulder and aimed his high beams back down the center line, cutting two feeble yellow cones into the mist.

There was a bump on the highway.

He wound down the window for a better look.

Was it moving?

He got out of the car as a shuddering wave struck the shore below. The tide was coming in. He walked into the road.

The bump was not moving. Only the fur ruffled in the breeze, as if combed by invisible fingers.

He bent down.

The blacktop was greased with blood and intestines, all that was left of a small animal. The legs were splayed and the body pressed into the pavement. The hindquarters were only a half-inch thick where his tire had rolled over it. The eyes were open, huge and shiny as marbles but now glazed with a rheumy film.

He had to move it. Otherwise it would be run over and over again until it became one of those things seen on roads everywhere, something so squashed and ruined that it is no longer recognizable.

He nudged the dead animal with his shoe. It was stuck to the asphalt. He kicked harder. It began to tear loose.

Then there was a flash behind him.

He turned, and was blinded as another pair of headlights rounded the curve.

He froze, targeted by the twin beams. A horn blasted as a bus closed the distance.

He raised his arms.

Stop!

Was he shouting? He could not hear his own voice. The roar of the bus came on and on.

At the last second he stepped aside. He lost his balance and fell backward in the wake.

The bus rolled past, barely missing his legs.

Then the horn blasted one more time and disappeared into the night.

He got up.

The bus had struck the creature again, flattening and crushing the remains.

Now he felt a throbbing in his foot.

He looked down, and saw an inch of tire tread imprinted across the end of one shoe.

There was a whispering in Eden Cove.

The sound might have come from the surf, from the traffic on the highway above, or from the restaurant, the Sand Dollar, at the edge of the private beach. He heard a desperate rustling in the oaks and Chinese elms near the lot as birds nested, hiding themselves from the night. But there was something more. It was a hissing, like a chorus of voices.

Martin tried not to listen.

The parking lot lights glared down through the windshield as he sat waiting for his breathing to return to normal. Now, with the engine off, the glass was streaked again. Under the artificial illumination the streaks congealed into a new and disturbing pattern: above the dashboard, an elongated appendage seemed to be reaching up through a background of amorphous shapes. Reflexively he raised his hand and drew on the steamed window, completing the picture, connecting the extension to the other half-formed masses. It resembled an arm in murky waters, too long and thin to be entirely human, grasping with thick webbed fingers. As Martin's breath came shallow and rapid the picture expanded to fill the windshield, and he saw what he had drawn. Abruptly he rubbed it out, bruising his knuckles against the cold glass.

He had come down the access road from the highway and into the parking lot. Now the road was nothing more than a narrow

52

tunnel barely visible between the trees next to the gatehouse.

The gatehouse . . .

Will might still be there. Sometimes he stayed on after closing time, sitting with his feet up and the lights off, listening to a talk radio station.

Was that where the voices were coming from?

Martin climbed out of the car.

"Will?"

He walked over and peered into the cramped wooden kiosk. There was just enough room inside for a desk and chair. He saw the empty cash drawer, the phone, the tide charts on the back wall. The door was padlocked from the outside.

Now the sounds of laughter and clinking glasses drifted over from the restaurant. Will was probably there, drinking at the bar. Martin considered joining him but could not bear the prospect of crowds and gawking faces. He turned away from the gatehouse and crossed the lot, making for the footpath that led down to the cabins.

When he was halfway across the lot, the back door of the restaurant opened and a Mexican cook came out carrying the garbage. The cook looked up, surprised to see anyone there.

Martin's eyes fixed on the bag, on the lumpy, distended contents that were trying to poke through.

The cook tossed the bag into a Dumpster and went back to the kitchen.

As the door closed, Martin cut across to the rear of the restaurant, overcome by a dreadful curiosity.

He grasped the battered steel lid of the Dumpster and forced it up.

Dark, shapeless mounds inside . . .

Then the kitchen door opened again, and the cook stood there with another bag.

If he asked me what I'm doing, Martin thought, what would I say? He saw himself as he would appear to others: filthy, disheveled, like one of the wandering homeless who sleep on the beaches and forage for spoiled food. He looked down at his hands. They were a dirty, sickly green under the sodium vapor lights.

He walked away, the cook's eyes on him, the whispering at his back louder than ever.

Will's cabin was beyond the untrimmed palm trees at the end of the path.

Once Eden Cove had served as a retreat for honeymoon couples and trysting celebrities. That time was long past, but the Cove retained an air of seedy exclusivity for those who owned or leased land here. There were cottages and guest houses and finally studio apartments that were little more than glorified sheds, arranged in diminishing grandeur along the tiered pathway to the beach. The area was surrounded by a windbreak of foliage that had propagated without restraint for several decades until the area resembled a compact jungle. The vegetation grew wild during spring and summer and then folded back on itself through the foggy months. Even now the verdant coloration and lush density remained, suggesting a coastal rain forest that contained all the ingredients of a closed ecosystem.

The homes became less imposing as the path descended, those with the most spectacular views commanding the highest prices, those nearest the eroding beach left to tenants with the least to lose. There were rumors that a once-famous film director lived in seclusion in the round, turreted mansion at the top. One house belonged to the skipper of the fishing charter, another to a retired teacher. A musician from the local bar band rented a mobile home on the windward side of the date palms. After that there was only a sandy dune above the beach and then Will's cabin, the last one this far down that was in habitable condition.

The cabin on the adjoining lot had fallen into disrepair and been demolished last year. A new residence was under construction by an unknown speculator, but work was now suspended until spring. A bare frame with plywood walls rose from a cement pallet, the wiring harnesses and PVC pipes yet to be connected. Already the exposed pine uprights had lost their rawness and darkened to the color of damp tree bark, with long black stains running down from the galvanized nailheads that held the boards together.

When Martin passed there was a hurried scrabbling beneath the partial roof, as though a lost animal had taken refuge within the half-finished enclosure.

Will had not been home.

The lights were off but the curtains were open. As Martin moved through the living room, he saw the cluttered furnishings outlined by a wet sheen, as though the tide had finally come all the way in to fill the room, submerging the house beneath luminous water. On the other side of the dune the ocean churned under a coating of pearly incandescence. Before the night was over it would shift to a warm oxidized patina, suggesting a fire in the sea. The red tide came each year like the turning of leaves, and left behind a scum the color of floating rust.

The kitchen sink glinted with stacks of unwashed dishes turning green under the subaquatic light. Now the old refrigerator shook and rattled as the noisy compressor started its cycle again, the motor sucking air before it built up torque and quieted into a steady hum. The vibration caused the plates to clatter. He heard a dish slide loose from the stack and crack against the porcelain, as the phone rang.

He ignored it.

The bell continued to ring. The caller, whoever it was, would not give up.

He retraced his steps through the dim living room and found the phone under a pile of clothes on the glass table. He lifted the receiver and held it without letting it touch his ear.

There was a rushing of white noise on the line, as from a seashell. Then a woman's voice:

"Will?"

He did not answer.

"Let me talk to Jack. I know he's there. They told me he left the police station an hour ago."

"Hello, Lee," he said.

"*Jack?* Are you all right?"

"I'm fine."

The white noise on the line again.

"Are you sure?"

"Does Captain Hook know you're calling?"

"That's none of your business," she snapped.

He heard her throat contract as she controlled herself. Then she went on in a detached, impersonal tone, like a stewardess or receptionist.

"One of the policemen showed me some wet clothing. He wanted to know if I could identify it."

"What did you tell him?"

"Nothing."

58

Did that mean she had lied for him? Or that she really didn't remember whose clothes they were?

"Thanks."

"Jack, what's going on? I heard about the body. It must have been awful. What were you doing there?"

"I wasn't spying on you, if that's what you mean."

"No, that's not what I mean. I wanted to know if you're in some kind of trouble, that's all."

"Don't worry. You don't have to get involved."

"I'm sorry I bothered!"

"Good-bye."

"Will you listen to me, Jack?" she said, trying one more time. "Is there anything I can do? If you need a lawyer . . ."

Her voice became high-pitched, like a girl's, and he realized with disbelief that she was about to cry.

She thinks I did it. She thought it the first time and she thinks it now.

"Good-bye, Lee."

"For God's sake, stop feeling sorry for yourself!"

He lowered the receiver. He heard the rising cheep of her voice from the earpiece.

"I had to leave for your sake as well as mine. We couldn't go on living together . . ."

He hung up.

He lay on the sofa and stared at the ceiling.

He could not sleep. As he sank deeper into the cushions, pictures took form in the blackness. He shut his eyes but they did not go away.

He sat up.

He leaned over the back of the sofa and pressed his forehead to the chill glass of the picture window. Tall grass shivered as sand blew in a flurry across the dunes. The waves appeared to be rushing the beach and receding at the same time, rolling in a wide line across his field of vision. Above the beach, the moon was shrunken and distant.

As he watched, it dropped out of the night sky and fell into the sea.

That was impossible.

He squeezed his eyes shut.

When he opened them, the moon was back where it belonged. But this time it hung above the waves for only a moment, then dipped down again, almost touching the surface, as the water began to ripple with the green-white glow of St. Elmo's fire.

He lay back.

I'm really tired, he thought.

The phosphorescent tide still roiled before his eyes, reflected on the ceiling, as if the room were inverted. He observed it without curiosity while the sound of the water lapped closer, penetrating the glass and entering the house.

Then a wedge of white light spilled out of the kitchen and across the end of the sofa.

"Hi, Will."

The refrigerator door closed, cutting off the light.

"Will . . . *who's there?*"

No answer.

He got up and crossed to the kitchen, in time to see what appeared to be a dwarf scurrying for the back door.

The dwarf could not turn the knob. Its short arms were loaded down with food. A carton of milk dropped to the floor. The contents sloshed over the linoleum and disappeared between the cracks.

Martin lunged, encircling the dwarf and lifting it off its feet. A piece of cheese, half a sandwich and fried chicken parts went flying. The stubby legs kicked frantically. When the heel of one shoe hit Martin in the ribs, he let go.

The dwarf grasped the doorknob again with tiny hands and threw itself forward. It was almost over the threshold when Martin tackled it.

He crawled onto the body and sat on the chest, reaching for the light switch.

"What the hell . . . ?"

It was not a dwarf but a child, a boy of six or seven, his face smudged with dirt and a look of terror contorting his features.

"Who are you?"

The boy became passive.

Martin waved a drumstick in front of the boy's eyes. "You don't have to steal from me. If you're that hungry . . ."

The boy suddenly flipped over and freed himself, pushed the door open and scooted out.

By the time Martin followed, he was gone.

Outside, branches and leaves moved. The surf was louder now, like a screenful of ball bearings. Somewhere beyond the shrubbery a dog barked.

The boy could be anywhere.

Martin started back inside.

Then he heard the creak of a board in the unfinished house next door.

Luminescent waves were visible through the disconnected studs. As Martin stepped between the beams, a tenpenny nail rolled across the cement, clinked against a joist and came to rest on the poured-concrete floor near his feet.

"Come on out," Martin said. "I'm not going to hurt you."

He entered the partially completed structure, following a maze of insulated pipes through the floorplan of a kitchen, a rectangular living area and a bathroom. He found the boy huddled in the corner of what would have been a small bedroom.

Martin held out his hand. "You don't have to be afraid."

The boy would not look at him. He remained hunkered in a tight ball, his arms around his knees, his face buried in his arms.

Martin came closer, kicking loose nails aside.

"Are you still hungry?"

When he touched him, the boy bolted.

Martin caught him at the other end of the foundation. The boy teetered, ready to jump down into the tall grass.

"Whoa . . . !"

He struggled to hold on until he was sure the child would not run again. He smelled salt perspiration on the boy's neck, mingled with the scent of old leaves. He felt a heart beating beneath his clasped hands.

The breeze came stronger off the ocean, stinking of decay and putrefaction. It blew the hair away from their foreheads. Above the waves the moon drifted sideways again. At last Martin realized that it was not the moon, after all, but a bird, a large white gull or pelican fishing the waters. And there was the hissing sound, separate and distinct from the surf and now very close by. It seemed to be coming from somewhere just beyond the boundaries of the house.

Holding the boy, he leaned over the edge.

He saw tufts of tall grass rooted in the dunes. The blades danced and rustled in the wind and darkened into a dense cross-hatching at sand level. As he watched, the roots moved. Lines the color of arterial blood swirled between the stalks, as if veins and capillaries were forming to join the acres of grass into one vast living organism.

There were hundreds, perhaps thousands of tiny garter snakes below, crawling over one another in a tangled mass. They were semitranslucent, like the red worms that appear on the banks of ponds after a rainfall.

That was where the whispering was coming from.

"Let's get out of here," Martin said.

He carried the boy away from the house and set him on his feet.

The boy slumped, resigned, as though ready to be led to his execution.

"What's your name?"

The boy put his chin to his chest.

"You must have a name. Mine's Jack."

The white light still shone from the back door of Will's house.

Martin led him inside to the refrigerator.

"All right, we'll eat first. Let's see. I've got eggs, ham . . ." He kicked a drumstick on the floor. "Too bad about the chicken."

The boy accepted a loaf of French bread and a jar of peanut butter. After the first sandwich he ignored the bread and ate the peanut butter straight off the spoon. Then he forgot about the spoon.

Martin stood aside and studied him. The boy's clothes were dirty and at least a size too small. His face was pale, his features not yet fully formed but handsome, his eyes dark and quick. He scraped the jar clean like a puppy at a bowl, afraid that each bite might be his last.

Martin found a can of Pepsi and set it in front of the boy. He opened a Dos Equis for himself.

"Now are you going to tell me who you are, or do I have to call the cops?"

The boy stopped drinking.

"You don't like cops, huh? Well, I'll tell you a secret—neither do I. Where do you live?"

The boy shot a glance through the open kitchen doorway at the house next door.

Martin remembered the home that had been there before, the one demolished last year. Who had lived in it? Will would know.

"Where are your mom and dad?"

The boy did not answer.

Martin took the empty peanut butter jar and dropped it in the trash.

"We'd better get you cleaned up, while I figure out what to do with you."

He walked him to the bathroom, turned on the light and was about to enter. He hesitated.

"There's the soap," he told the boy. "And a towel. I'll wait for you. Okay?"

He closed the door and went to the living room. He put the lamp on and sat down and drank the rest of his beer.

As far as he knew there were no children in residence at the Cove. Where's Will? he thought. He'd know what to do.

When he heard water splashing, he got up uneasily and returned to the bathroom.

"All right in there?"

Only the splashing.

He opened the door.

The boy had his head down in the sink. He was drinking directly from the faucet. Martin was relieved that there was no water in the tub.

He rubbed the towel over the boy's face.

"That's good enough, I guess. Now what do you say we get some real food?"

They started up the path.

The boy watched the bushes, alert at every turn.

"What are you afraid of?" Martin asked him.

The boy said nothing.

They passed oversized chrysanthemums and bird-of-paradise plants and were about to make the last turn up to the restaurant, when a shadow fell across their path.

Martin shaded his eyes against the parking lot lights. There was the outline of a man. Backlight flared around the silhouette, obscuring the features.

"Will?"

He was surprised to feel the boy's hand in his. The palm was hot and moist. The boy squeezed Martin's fingers.

"It's okay," Martin told him. "He's one of the good guys."

As the shadow descended, the boy let go of his hand and ran into the bushes.

Martin went after him. He parted the bushes and saw the boy cowering on the ground, hugging his knees again. He managed to get one arm under the legs. This time the boy resisted with the infinite mass of dead weight. Martin put his other arm around the torso and lifted.

The boy kicked and flailed. A sharp elbow caught Martin in the Adam's apple. He let go.

Now he was out of patience. He grabbed the boy before he could run and pulled him down. Then he sat on him and pinned him with his knees. He held the chin and forced the boy to look at him.

"You think I'm going to hurt you? Is that what you think?"

The boy's eyes rolled up and fixed on the tall shadow that stood over them.

"Give me a hand, Will," Martin said. "It's a long story . . ."

A metal blade glinted like burnished silver.

"Go ahead," said a voice. "I'd like to hear it."

The pincer flexed, snapping open and shut, open and shut.

"I came here to tell you to stay away from Lee, you sorry son of a bitch. Now I wish to Christ I had a camera. I guess it's true what they say about this place. Who's that, your punk?"

Steven chuckled mirthlessly, the hook flashing and snipping.

"You ought to let me do you a favor—cut it off and hang it up to dry!"

Martin let go of the boy and went for Steven's throat.

There was a scream from above.

At the top of the path, another shadow towered in silhouette. The boy thrashed as the shadow caught him.

"Chris," said the shadow, "is it you?"

"Down here, Will," Martin called. "Hold him for me."

The boy followed Will down the hillside without protest.

"You fucking perverts," said Steven won-deringly.

Will looked at the man with the claw. "Who's your friend?"

"He's no friend," said Martin.

"Back off," Steven said to Will. "I was just going to teach this faggot here a lesson."

"You have a dirty mouth," Will said, "you know that?"

"This is private."

The metal blade clicked.

Will stepped behind him, forcing the artifi-cial arm into a chicken-wing.

"Drop it."

"Fuck you."

"I said—"

"I can't!"

"You want to be careful with that thing. You might hurt yourself."

"Let me go," said Steven, "or I'll sue your mother-fucking ass off!"

Will saw that the blade was attached and loosened his grip. He laughed. "Pretty tough, aren't you? For a gimp."

"It's all right," Martin said. "He's harm-less."

Steven brushed himself off, then started up the path, glaring at Martin.

"Just remember what I said, asshole!

From now on, you are definitely on my shit list!''

When he was gone, Will's face split in a crooked grin.

"Is that guy for real?"

"Lee thinks so."

"You mean *that's* the shithead? I should have broken his other arm!"

Martin looked around. The boy was with them, standing as close as possible to Will.

"You know each other?"

"Sure," said Will, laying an arm around the boy's shoulders. "He used to live next door to me. Right, Chris?"

The boy nodded.

Does he talk, too? Martin wondered.

"So what are you doing back here?" Will asked. "Where's your mother?"

The boy started to cry.

Martin gazed past them, as the seascape below the path changed color. It was as if an endless quantity of blood were now emptying into the ocean, turning it bright red.

Part Two
The Big Sky

4.

Lissa Shelby stood in darkness, trying to see through the window.

The only object she could make out was the intercom box on this side.

My eyes are getting worse, she thought.

She touched the switch. The intercom crackled, then whined feedback. Quickly she released the switch, hoping that Dr. Underwood had not heard. The psychiatrist had a strict policy about observers.

She moved close to the window. Her breath on the glass only made it harder to tell what was going on through the granular darkness. She rubbed out a spot on the aluminized pane.

The image was a blur.

It's time to stop kidding myself. I really do need glasses . . .

She found the volume control and turned it lower. Then she flipped the intercom switch again.

There was the sound of a chair scraping.

She lowered her head, listening intently.

"Ruthie," said Dr. Underwood's voice, "what happened to the little girl?"

"She fell down."

"Why?"

"She runned away."

"I see. Why did she run away?"

"Because."

"Can't you tell me? Please?"

"Because *he* chased her."

Lissa raised her head. Her eyes had begun to adjust. Now she saw what looked like shapes at the bottom of a dim fishtank, murky and abstract. She closed her eyes for relief and gray phosphenes fired on her retinas. Then she opened her lids again. The grainy shadows came together and at last she was able to see a pattern through the two-way mirror.

A preschool girl sat on the floor, next to a Raggedy Ann doll. Behind her the legs of an upended chair pointed like spokes at the ceiling.

76

"Why?" asked Dr. Underwood.

"You know."

"No, I don't."

"The *man*."

"What man?"

"*Him*."

"What's his name?"

"He doesn't have a name."

"What does he look like?"

"I don't know."

"I'll bet you do."

"No, I don't."

"Well, who does?"

"Nobody."

"You mean nobody's ever seen him?"

"Sure they have."

"Don't they know what he looks like?"

"No."

"Why not?"

"Because."

"Because why?"

"Because he doesn't have a face."

"Okay, tell me about this . . . man with no face."

"He's bad."

"What does he do?"

"Hurts people."

"Who? Who does he hurt?"

"Kids."

"Can you show me how, Ruthie?"

With a sudden wrenching motion the girl took the doll and wrung its neck.

"Like that!"

"Did he do that to you?"

"He wants to."

"How do you know?"

"Everybody knows what he does."

Ruthie swung the doll again and again, striking it against the floor. The button eyes flew off and stuffing protruded from the stomach.

"There!" said Ruthie. "See what he did?"

"But why?" said the doctor.

"Because he's the *Man With No Face!*"

The doctor got up from his chair.

"That's all for today, Ruthie . . ."

Lissa snapped to. How long had she been standing here? For the entire session? She could not read her watch.

Behind her, the door to the hall creaked open.

"How's it going, Lees?"

She whirled around. "Bill!"

"What are you doing in here?"

His voice was ironic and accusatory, as always. She saw the thatch of stringy hair outlined against the hall, the twin circles of his John Lennon glasses shining opaquely.

"I—I was . . ."

Why did she feel guilty? It was his tone, as if he had caught her in a secret ritual. Does he talk to everyone that way? she wondered. Or is it only me?

The intercom box sputtered as Dr. Underwood cleared his throat on the other side of the mirror.

She turned in time to see the doctor approach the window. His eyes narrowed as he stared into the silvered glass. He seemed to be looking directly at her.

"Close the door, Bill," she whispered.

"Huh?"

"For God's sake . . ." She reached around him and drew the door shut on the light from the hallway.

Dr. Underwood left the window.

"Let's go, Ruthie. Time for lunch."

He paused at the side wall of the play-therapy room, his finger on the light switch. A child's oversized drawing was tacked to the cork panels. It showed a crude house and a family of stick figures, trees, flowers, a car. But something was missing. Then she realized what it was. *There was no sun in the sky.* Below the drawing, modular shelves supported a menagerie of dolls and stuffed animals that stared back at the two-way mirror.

Lissa squirmed like a pinned butterfly. The doctor turned off the light, plunging both rooms into darkness.

"I think he saw you," said Bill with a chuckle.

She felt his breath on her hair. She backed up, fumbling for the intercom box. She threw the switch and the white noise stopped.

"What do you want, Bill?"

"Uh, you got a phone call, Lees. Didi was paging you. I guess you couldn't hear."

"Thanks," she said.

Instead of opening the door and letting her out, he took another step toward her.

"You never answered my question," he said.

"I beg your pardon?"

"What are you doing in here?"

"I was observing."

"Oh yeah? Who's the subject?"

"Her name is Ruthie J." Is that all she is, Lissa thought, the subject? Is that all any of the children are to you? "They admitted her yesterday."

Bill's rubber soles squeaked as he moved in. She made herself keep talking as she attempted to get to the door without bumping into him.

"She's on my caseload. I'm supposed to counsel her tomorrow. Monday, I mean."

"Nobody knows where you are," said Bill. "You're not on the chart today. But I saw you come in."

"I'm glad," she said. "Now if you don't mind . . ."

She took a chance and steered left, ran into the wall and slid along it, searching for the door. She grappled with the knob. Bands of fluorescent light streamed in, reflected off the olive-drab enamel of the hallway.

Bill followed her out.

"Speaking of lunch," he said.

Who? What was he talking about? The doctor. The doctor and Ruthie were going to lunch. If Bill had heard any of it, that was the only part that had registered with him.

She clipped down the hallway, hoping to lose him.

"I was thinking," he said behind her. "I'm off this afternoon . . ."

Spare me, she thought.

"Not today, Bill," she said. "I'd better get that call now, okay?"

She pushed through the double doors at the end of the corridor. The sky outside was considerably dimmer than the ceiling fixtures indoors. Her arms felt cold, lifeless un-

81

der the dove-gray overcast. She rubbed them, expecting the outer layer of skin to roll up under her fingernails. She hurried along the covered walkway and into the next building.

Bill tracked her as relentlessly as a dog in an orphanage.

"If this is your day off," he said, "why did you come in?"

"I wanted to see the file on Ruthie J."

"What for?" He was genuinely baffled. "You have enough to do without worrying about one more brat, am I right?"

They passed the Senior Girls' Infirmary. On the other side of the chickenwire glass, she recognized Deb and Stacey and Kirsten seated disconsolately on the edges of the cots, thermometers drooping from their lips. Lissa knocked on the window. They waved.

"Have you seen the pop sheet?" she said.

"What about it?"

"The population at the hall is up a hundred percent this month. And it's still climbing. Don't you wonder why?"

"Runaways," said Bill.

"So many, just like that?"

"The weather, probably."

"The weather's always like this."

82

"Well, you know teenagers. When they're bored, they get into trouble."

"That's just it," she said. "The new admissions aren't teens—they're all Juniors. There aren't that many little kids who run away from home, at least not around here, and when they do they're sent back right away. These are being held, because they need help. That's the only explanation."

As she passed the Senior Girls' residence rooms, she glanced into each one. Most of the beds were empty. That meant they were already at first lunch.

"You know what I think, Lissa? I think you worry too much. We do what we can. Anything more, for what they pay us . . ."

She came to the end of the corridor and faced him.

"Let me ask you something, Bill. Did you see this morning's newspaper?"

"You mean the body on the beach?"

"It wasn't just a body." Can't you put two and two together? she thought. "It was another child. A very young child. This one had been mutilated."

"Maybe it was a shark attack."

"There have never been sharks off the Point as long as I've lived here." She seethed with impatience. "Something's going on in

83

this town, and the kids, the little ones, they know about it, and they're scared out of their minds. That's what *I* think.''

She pushed against the next set of double doors before he could answer.

At the entrance to the Junior Girls' Cottage, she saw that the corridor was empty, with none of the usual activity she had come to expect. Where are they? she thought. Second lunch isn't for another half-hour.

Then she thought: *They're hiding.*

She hesitated, her hand on the door. Superimposed over the hallway ahead was the reflection of Bill's dead-white face in the glass. He was scratching his goatee.

"Sometimes I just don't get you, Lissa."

"Don't worry about it," she said. "It's not you, Bill. You're very sweet. Really, you are." It's a matter of time, she thought. And energy. I don't have enough of either. "Ask me again next week? I may have some answers by then."

He nodded as if he understood, flashed her one of his knowing smirks, and wandered off across the grass in the direction of the Senior Boys' wing. Looking for someone else to rub up against, she thought.

Well, it ain't me, babe.

Why can't I just tell him to screw off? It

would be easier in the long run. But that might hurt him. It would be unkind.

Junior Girls' was cold as a tomb. She saw Fitz with his feet up under the TV in the dayroom. The toys were all neatly stacked on the shelves and the four-square balls were still in the bin.

"What happened to the heat?" she asked.

"Nothin'," said Fitz. "Hi, Lees."

"Hi, Fitz. Where is everybody?"

"Early nap time today. They didn't want to play."

"Why not?"

Fitz shrugged his massive shoulders. "Don't axe me. You know that new desal— desalinization plant? I hear they're puttin' out negative ions."

"Positive," she said.

"Say what?"

"Positive ions. Negative are okay."

"Whatever. All I know is, they're the bad kind. When you can't even get little kids to go out and play, the whole town must be ready to pack it in."

She took a moment to look into the Junior Girls' rooms. In one, a stiff, ashen leg was sticking out from beneath a McKenzie Hall blanket. She lifted it and found two little girls together on one mattress, sleeping like spoons. Gently she moved the leg away from the edge and tucked the covers under the springs.

"Hey, Lees?" said Fitz from around the corner. "Didi was looking for you."

"I know," she said. "Fitz?"

"Yeah?"

"Keep an eye on these two, will you?"

"How come?"

"I think they're having a bad dream."

She left the Junior Girls' Cottage and went on to the O.D.'s office.

With any luck Underwood would still be in the cafeteria. What if he came back to pick up his messages while she was there? He would have plenty to say to her. Assuming, of course, that he had seen her through the therapy room mirror. She would have to confront him at her briefing on Monday, but at least she'd have the rest of the weekend to put together a theory that made sense. She needed more facts. It was important; it mattered.

The Officer of the Day's desk was loaded with file folders. Didi hunched over her type-writer, filling in the new admissions forms.

"There you are, girl." Didi clicked her

tongue. "What you doing here on Saturday? You sure must need the overtime."

"Do you have a message for me?"

She handed Lissa a WHILE YOU WERE OUT slip.

"Say, who's Will? You didn't tell me about him."

Lissa examined the slip. The URGENT box had been checked. Under the telephone number Didi had written (*from the Cove*). Lissa smiled.

"Which phone can I use?"

"In the big office," said Didi. "Line two."

She let herself in and closed the door. The blinds were open but that didn't help much. On the walls were the charts for Tiger and Lion and Chipmunk Cottages, the behavior mod graphs and meal schedules and shift rosters. Weak bars of light fell across the desk, barely adequate for her to dial.

"Will?" she said into the phone. "Lissa Shelby . . . Hi yourself! How are you, Big Red?"

The radial tires of her Datsun screamed as she turned into the underground garage and found her parking space. The cars on either side of her were much newer, their tops like hard candy that has been left out in the rain, the hoods marbled with watermarks. The parking structure was supposed to provide protection against the elements, but dampness crept in and condensed every night, leaving the metallic paint crenelated in a pattern that reminded her of snail tracks.

She gathered up her files and started upstairs.

On the way, she noticed how the metal had bubbled and begun to rust around the bottom edges of a Volvo station wagon. She was afraid to look back at her own car. Would she climb in one morning only to feel the frame of the Datsun break apart and crumble under her?

As she entered the apartment complex, a large cat ran across the gravel path in front of her.

"Here, kitty . . . !"

It was the fat black Persian from 6–A. The cat twitched its whiskers, bared sharp teeth and hissed, then ran over to the ivy. A faint mewling came from the heart-shaped leaves, and two tiny blue eyes peered out at her.

"Is that your baby, Idi? Good girl!"

The mother cat picked up her kitten by the scruff of the neck, carried it to the cinder block wall and sprang. In one fluid motion both cats were up and over.

Lissa stood on her toes at the wall. She saw Idi and the kitten bounding across the field under a sky the color of crushed pearls, toward the abandoned drive-in at the edge of the salt flats.

Do Judy and Jeff know she's out? she wondered. If they're not careful that kitten will grow up wild, like an animal in the wilderness. Cats revert if you don't keep them inside. I'd better call or stop by . . .

Or should I? The little one has her mother to take care of her. Maybe that's enough.

She returned to the gravel path, and tried not to think about her work.

By the time she got to her apartment she felt empty and marvelous, despite everything. She had the rest of Saturday and all day Sunday ahead of her. A blank slate. Except for Will from Eden Cove . . . She did not know him well, only from the jokes they shared at the gatehouse whenever she stopped by the Sand Dollar for lunch. She had trouble remembering his face. But she looked forward to the visit, however unexpected.

I wonder what he wants to talk to me about?

He arrived a little after four. She buzzed him up, finished mixing a bowl of guacamole, set it out next to the chips and went to the door.

When she opened it, a man she had never seen before was standing there with a child in his arms.

The child was not moving. Without thinking she reached out to help. "Is he all right? Let me . . ."

Will was farther back on the landing, about to knock on the wrong door.

"Lee-za! *There* you are."

"Will, what—?"

"That's Chris. He's a sleepyhead. And this is my friend Jack."

"Hello." She shifted the boy onto her shoulder. His eyes were closed but he was warm. She remembered to breathe again. "Well, don't just stand there."

She led them into her living room.

"I hope you don't mind messes," she said, suddenly self-conscious. She handed the child to Will and cleared the couch.

Will laid the boy down. "He fell asleep in the car. The little guy had a rough night."

"Is he yours, Big Red?"

"God, what a thought."

His friend took off his jacket and covered the child's legs.

"You must think I'm a slob." She saw the room through their eyes and was overcome with embarrassment. She cleared the chairs and opened the bedroom door just enough to dump the files, hoping they couldn't see around her. "Actually, I am. Now you know my secret. I'm sorry . . . Would either of you like something to drink?"

Will held up a six-pack of Dos Equis. "I'll put these in the freezer. Where's the kitchen?"

"Over there."

He winked and disappeared into the next room with a hipster's shuffle. The short salt-and-pepper hair always threw her. It didn't go with the long, lean body, the jeans hanging low on his hips, the twinkle in his eye. Now she was even more confused. Was this a social call? He hadn't said anything about bringing anyone with him.

"Do you live in the Cove, too?" she asked the other man.

"What?"

"Eden Cove," she said.

"Not really." He hovered in a holding pattern near the overstuffed chair.

"Oh."

He was not unpleasant looking, a few indeterminate years younger than Will, with uncombed brown hair and downcast eyes. There was a tentative quality to his presence in the apartment, as though he was not sure he wanted to be here, as though he did not know where he wanted to be. His cotton trousers were faded and unpressed, his long-sleeved shirt clean but full of wrinkles from the Laundromat.

"Have you known Will a long time?"

He took so long to answer that Lissa started to get spooked.

"He was my best man," he said finally.

To break the tension, she picked up a throw pillow and crossed to the couch. The child was sleeping so fitfully that she was reluctant to place it under his head.

"This one must be yours, then."

"No, I—I don't have any children." She noticed a tic pulling at the corner of one eye.

Will came back into the room.

Lissa said, "Sorry I haven't been by this week. They've got me on a new schedule."

"I noticed." Will winked.

On the couch, the boy stirred.

92

"So." She kept her voice down. "Are you going to tell me about your little friend?"

Will sighed. "I hate to lay this on you. But I don't know who else to ask."

The other man—Jack?—looked at the floor.

The boy curled into a fetal position, his knees under his chin. She had seen that posture before, at the Hall.

She motioned Will to a sliding glass door, and he followed her out onto the small balcony.

"What's on your mind, Will?"

"You work at McKenzie Hall, right?"

"You know that. You called me, remember?"

"What's it like there?"

The lines around his eyes were hard and set; the funny, jokey manner was gone. She had never seen him like this.

"Well," she said carefully, vamping until she could be sure of his meaning, "it's a placement facility. What can I tell you? We get kids from all over the area—abuse cases, those who need protection, that sort of thing. They go home eventually, or to foster parents. What's your point?"

Will's face, weathered from years at the beach, tightened with conflicting emotions.

93

"Jesus, I don't want to bust the little guy."

So that's it, she thought. "That's Juvenile Hall, the Sheriff's Department. We're DPSS."

"You think he'd know the difference?"

"Start at the beginning. Who is he?"

"His name's Chris. Christopher Buckley. He used to live at the Cove. They moved away last year. Something heavy must have happened to him, because he showed up last night, alone. He won't talk. All I know is, he's scared out of his gourd."

Lissa had guessed that part, but hearing it grabbed her like a cry in the night.

"Where does he live now?"

"Nobody knows. There was no forwarding address. I found some Buckleys in the phone book, but not the right ones."

"I might be able to trace the parents through County Services."

"The father's dead. The mother was handicapped, the way I remember it."

"Then she'll be on the welfare rolls. Did you try that?"

"Yeah. The County offices are closed till Monday. Schools, too."

There was the burden of unfamiliar responsibility on his face, and the pain of genu-

94

ine concern. Bless him, she thought. He has a good heart. I can see it in his eyes.

"Tell me what you want to do," she said.

"That's what we need to talk about. What's the procedure?"

"You have to file a complaint with the Department of Public Social Services. I can help with that. Then they send someone to interview the parents . . ."

"If they can find them."

"In that case, he automatically becomes a ward of the court."

And gets thrown in with the orphans and transients, she thought, the ones who wet the bed and moan in their sleep, the ones who know they are not wanted.

Above the balcony the sky darkened, as if a dimmer had been turned down on the other side of a frosted glass bowl.

"Give me a couple of days," she said. "I can't promise anything. But I'll try to come up with an alternative. Maybe I can locate the mother. Meanwhile, keep him at the Cove and . . ."

"What does the law say about that?"

"You don't want to know."

"That's what I figured. What do I do if he runs again? We're dealing with one shit-scared little boy here."

"He won't tell you what happened?"

"Not a word. Ask Jack. He found him."

She glanced in at the other man. He had moved to the couch and now sat with one arm resting across the boy to comfort him in case he woke up. They both looked like refugees, lost and forgotten.

"I guess we've got a problem, don't we, Big Red?"

"Not you. Me."

She leaned her elbows on the wrought-iron railing and gazed out over the other apartments in the enclosed complex, the manicured grounds, the planters and cheerful curtains, the landscaped walkway to the pool, all the cleverly-disguised fortifications against the encroaching night. What about those who don't have a place to hide? They're left to fend for themselves, even children. Why are they out there while I'm in here? It doesn't make sense.

What were the alternatives? There weren't any. There was a child in her living room who needed help. It was as simple as that.

Somebody has to do something.

It starts here.

"You can leave him with me."

There, I've said it. It's what he wants. He's too decent to come right out and ask.

Will shook his head adamantly. "No way."

"Be serious. What other way is there?"

"I had to be sure. I'll drive him over to the Hall. They have psychiatrists, right?"

"Yes." Underwood, she thought. Ten minutes a week, if he's lucky. "But let's talk about this some more . . . I think I'm ready for one of those beers. How about you?"

"You got it."

"There's food," Lissa called after him, "if you guys—"

The boy on the couch moaned, kicked the jacket off his legs.

Will put a finger to his lips.

She went in.

"We'd better move him," she said to Jack.

He nodded.

The bedroom, was that the only place? It was, God help her. "I can do it."

But Jack was already lifting him, cradling the head against his chest.

Oh, well, she thought, at least he's nobody I know. It doesn't matter what he thinks. She picked up the jacket and showed the way.

"In here."

She directed him through an obstacle course to the bed. Her room was a repository for the unordered and unfinished business of her life. Stacks of paperwork rose from the floor like stalagmite growths below the jumbled gallery of yellowed and curling children's drawings she had taped to every available inch of the walls. The drawings fluttered like a flock of sleeping bats disturbed by their passing. They set the boy on the bed and covered him with a comforter.

The last light of day penetrated the window shade, revealing a pale, angelic face centered on her down pillow. She pushed the hair away from the closed eyelids, the meshed lashes.

Jack was examining the drawings on the walls. Absorbed, he smoothed out a cracked tempera of a grinning lion. FOR LISSA, read the caption. I LOVE YOU! MARCIE.

"They're not exactly works of art," she whispered. "But I can't bring myself to throw them away."

"This one is good. Marcie has a nice line."

"Are you an artist?"

"Just commercial work," he said.

His profile was striking, the broad forehead under the fall of hair, the straight nose, the full lips and strong chin.

"Some of these kids," she said, "meant a lot to me. I don't know what happened to Marcie. She'd be thirteen now. And that one—" She pointed to a fingerpaint waterfall. "Bobby B. grew up to be a drug addict. I hear he's living in a halfway house. The pictures don't change, though. That's why I love them."

He nodded respectfully and moved along the wall.

"Will said you found him."

"That's right."

"Do you know what happened?"

"I wish I did. Something sure scared him."

"There's a lot of that going around."

"Is there?" He turned with interest, very close to her.

"Where I work, they call it the Man With No Face." Ruthie J., she thought. That's it. Or rather it's a start. I wonder how many kids know about it?

"The what?"

"It's like the boogeyman, I guess."

Next to them, something brushed against the door.

"Hello?"

Will handed in two bottles of beer. Behind him, the TV set was on in the living room.

"I wanted to catch the score," he said. "Do you mind, Lissa?"

"Of course not. Did you see the chips? I have glasses . . ."

Will drifted back to the TV and the game, leaving the volume low.

In the kitchen, she took down glasses from the cupboard.

"Don't bother," said Jack.

"Are you sure?"

She poured her own bottle into a glass. Ice had formed around the neck and needlelike crystals floated on the foam. Her lips stung when she tasted it.

In the living room, the crowd cheered in a soft hiss.

"You and Will must be old friends."

"A while. He was the only person I knew when I moved here."

"The Cove?"

"Shadow Bay. My wife—my ex-wife . . ."

She saw him withdraw, his eyes lowered.

"Sorry," she said. "I guess I put my foot in it."

"No, you didn't."

She sought to change the subject. "You say you're in commercial art? That must be interesting."

"It must be." He chugged half of his bottle. When he came up for air, he leaned back expansively against the tile countertop, as though willing himself out of his shell. "I started out to be an artist. Then my wife got pregnant, we needed a bigger house, and with what I was earning . . ."

"You don't have to explain."

"It's all right. You asked a question, and you deserve an answer."

He seemed to want to have this conversation. When was the last time he talked to a woman? she wondered.

"How long have you been divorced?"

"You don't want to hear any of this." He drained the bottle, saw that it was empty and looked around the kitchen in a panic.

She took the other bottles out of the freezer and handed him one.

He popped it open immediately, sending the cap jittering across the floor.

"I'm a good listener," she said.

"I had a little girl. She was eighteen months old. One day I gave her a bath. I left the room for a minute, and when I came back she had fallen down in the water and drowned. That was that. Lee never forgave me."

His eyes were pink now. His expression did not change, his features frozen in a pattern that would not give him away. Only his eyes betrayed him.

She touched his arm.

He pulled back, startled.

101

"I don't know why I told you that," he said.

She took his chin in the V of her hand and forced it back up.

"You needed to tell someone."

"You don't even know me."

"Sometimes that makes it easier."

She put her arms out and hugged him. She held him until the shaking stopped. Then she released him abruptly, shocked at herself.

In the living room, a thin, reedy voice was saying:

"... *A Department of Water and Power worker discovered the body in a storm drain early this morning. So far, the victim's identity* ..."

She hurried to the TV set.

"Jesus," said Will, "can you believe it? They found another one." He increased the volume.

The local news anchor sat at his desk, a chroma-keyed view of an alley onscreen behind him. The camera panned to follow a sheeted body on a gurney. The body was very small. Police officers conferred at the rear of a building, next to a Dumpster.

"Anyone with any information should contact ..."

"The Man With No Face," said Lissa.

Will looked at her. "Who?"

"Don't you get it? He's not the boogeyman. He's real!"

Across the room, the front door slammed.

"Chris . . . ?" said Will.

The bedroom door stood open.

He heard, she thought, slapping the TV off. And what we said—what I said. He woke up, and heard, and ran. What have I done?

Jack was already out the front door.

As Will rushed after him, she went out onto the balcony and leaned over the railing. She heard footfalls below. They could have been coming from anywhere.

Will emerged onto the gravel path.

"Which way?" he yelled up at her.

"I don't know!"

"Stay there," he told her, and ran off between the buildings.

She scanned the path in both directions, then looked over the ramparts of the development to the surrounding field. Outside the walls, low marshlands extended all the way to the coast highway, with only the dingy white screen of the empty drive-in theater to interrupt a clear view of the sea. As soon as the real estate people had their way, those fenced-off acres would make way for more condo apartments. The Big Sky was out of

103

business, but the owner refused to sell the remaining parcel. . . .

Now a distant figure was running breakneck across the flats, toward the only other shelter in sight, as a diffused sun sank behind the empty movie screen. Was it Jack? Or the boy?

"There!" she shouted. "There he is!"

No one heard her.

5.

A few broken letters clung to the old marquee despite the ravages of time and the elements:

ALL ARS 99¢
O EN AT DUSK
RING TH   HOLE FAMILY!

Martin ran for the drive-in.

He could not see the boy, but there was a clanging from the entrance driveway. By the time he got there a padlocked chain was swinging back and forth against the gate.

Now he heard the patter of feet inside the fence.

He hooked his fingers in the links of the gate and pushed. The chain held it from opening more than eight inches, not wide enough for him to squeeze through. He cupped his hands around his mouth.

"Christopher!"

The only answer was the hissing of the sea.

He took a good look at the hurricane fence. He could throw his jacket over the barbed wire on top, get a running start and scale it, drop down on the other side . . .

If he had his jacket.

There had to be a break somewhere in the fence. It curved away in either direction. Which way? To the south was the exit drive, protected by sawtoothed spikes. DO NOT ENTER, warned the sign, SEVERE DAMAGE TO TIRES. To the north, only the night.

The boy could be on his way out the other side by now, headed for the highway or the beach. If so they might never find him.

Martin ran full-bore at the exit gate, despite his foot, leaping over the spikes and up onto the fence. Cloth ripped and the barbed wire tore his palms but there was no time for the pain. Then he was over and down, his legs bending to take the impact.

Breathing hard, he stood up behind a small building.

The doorways to the restrooms were dark. In the men's room, high windows admitted a last trace of illumination from the low cloud cover outside. There were no doors on the stalls. Passing the discolored mirror over the basin, he froze at the image of a wild-haired man by one of the toilets. Then he recognized his own reflection and the open cubicle behind him.

In the women's room, a shadow was visible under the last partition. He kicked the stall door open as a rat tiptoed around the peeling toilet seat and hid behind the raised lid, its hairless tail hanging down into the dry porcelain bowl. A pair of empty shoes rested at the base of the commode, high heels touching. What had become of the owner?

He checked out the snack bar on the other side of the building.

The menu board advertised nachos and soda and microwave hamburgers. The hot dog machine was empty, with bare metal prongs sticking out from the rotisserie like the rays of a medieval halo. Within the display case a single box of Milk Duds remained, a hole gnawed through the cardboard. The condiments were long gone except for a cracked residue at the bottom of the stainless steel ketchup well. An overlooked five-gallon popcorn bag lay slumped in the corner, stale puffed kernels leaking out of an incision across the front. As Martin left the snack bar, the bag moved. More popcorn tumbled out and another hairless tail burrowed through a hole in the plastic. He backed off, disgusted, and felt something brush against his leg.

A fat black cat ran past him and pounced. After a quick thrashing the squeals died down. Then the cat emitted a warbling signal and a kitten showed itself at the edge of the counter, tail held high. It played with the popcorn until the big cat swatted its ear and directed its attention to the kill.

The popcorn was bait, Martin realized. The cat had left some of it uneaten to serve a greater purpose. Whenever a rat or mouse appeared, the cat was ready to spring its trap.

The kitten's lucky to have a mother like that, he thought.

He moved on.

The drive-in lot consisted of a few paved acres, built up into raked rows to lift the front wheels of cars to the right viewing angle, crisscrossed by speaker posts. Below the screen was a playground area with swings, a slide, a merry-go-round and a sandbox. The surface of the screen was mottled by rain damage and the scars of countless hurled bottles that had left indentations the size of fists in the unpatched panels. The tilted easel was several stories high, an off-white canvas waiting for something to be drawn on it.

He heard feet running again, closer this time.

"Chris?"

The sound came from somewhere among the speaker posts. There were hundreds of them, each with a shadow pooled at its base. Some of the dangling cords seemed to be moving in the breeze . . .

Except that there was no breeze.

He climbed the wooden stairs at the side of the building for a better look. Halfway up, his foot slipped off a rickety board and he nearly fell. It was his bad shoe. The end was peeling open where the bus had run over it. There was no feeling in the toes. He dragged himself higher, his entire foot now numb.

The view from the top was only a little better. He could see all of the lot, but most of the fence was lost in shadow. When he shifted his weight onto his good leg the boards creaked under him. He was about to start back down, when he heard a scratching on the other side of the projection booth door.

"Is anybody there?"

He felt his way in, leaving the door open. When his eyes adjusted he saw a tall mass against one wall. It was a stack of film cans that clattered hollowly when he touched them, leaving a smear of wet fingermarks on the rusted steel lids. His hands were bleeding.

Strips of broken celluloid hung from a hook on the wall, the tail ends poised over a trash barrel. He peered down and saw more coiled lengths of discarded film. He did not reach into the dark tangle.

The projectors were still at the windows. They were huge old machines with ventilation ducts connecting the lamp housings to the ceiling. Why had such expensive equipment been left behind? Because they were so heavy? Or did the owner hope to reopen the drive-in one day, when the fog lifted?

Martin looked through the window. The glass was occluded with dust and crystallized salt, but he could see most of the grounds below. Christopher might be down there somewhere, hiding in the shadows.

If only there were more light . . .

On the wall near his elbow was a button marked POWER.

He pushed it.

110

He was not surprised when nothing happened. The electricity would have been disconnected long ago.

He left the window, and bumped into another piece of equipment. It rose only to waist level, but it was longer and broader than the other machines. There was a two-stroke motor with fuel tank, a fan belt, a 12-gauge extension cord that was plugged into the projectors.

A generator.

Of course. For backup in case of a power failure.

He pulled the ripcord. The motor turned over with a shuddering tremor, releasing the sweet, nasty fumes of old gasoline. He yanked harder. The valves coughed and sputtered. The third time the generator backfired and caught. The floor shook and rumbled under the vibration.

He pushed the POWER button again.

At the window, there was a flash of lightning.

Martin put his nose to the glass.

Outside, lights flickered, dimmed, flashed again, and finally held.

There were tall poles around the perimeter of the lot. At the top of each pole was a mercury vapor fixture. Now the bulbs blazed

111

brilliantly, drawing power from the generator.

The motor banged and wheezed, sucking dirty gas from the tank. There couldn't be much left. At any moment it would die for good and the darkness would return.

He wiped the window with his sleeve.

A hundred yards away, something moved in the temporary daylight.

"Chris, stay where you are!"

He was shouting through glass.

He lunged against it with his shoulder. The window shattered and sharp icicles fell to the ground in front of the snack bar.

Now he saw the bars of the merry-go-round turning, strobing the bottom of the bright screen. Near the sandbox, the chains of a swing jerked and slowed.

Martin descended the stairs, forcing his bad foot to support him. The numbness was creeping up his ankle to the rest of his leg. He hit the cement awkwardly and threw himself forward between the rows of speakers.

The playground was hundreds of feet away. Already the swings had stopped moving and the carousel was clocking down to a crawl. He used the speaker posts for support. Slotted metal boxes toppled off their stands like praying mantis heads and fell around him, striking at his legs, then snapped back on their cords before they could touch the ground. He started to lose his balance, windmilled his arms and fought to stay upright as he hurtled forward.

At the end of the row, a dark shape cast an elongated shadow across the screen.

"Wait!" he cried.

An arm showed at the side of the white surface, swinging in semaphore fashion, as if waving him on. Then it withdrew, as the generator shut down and the cleaning lights went off and the night fell again.

His leg failed him completely. He stumbled into the sandbox and grabbed the bottom of the hazy whitewashed screen. It was hard and chalky. He felt it vibrate like the membrane of a giant drum, pulsing with the tide and the throb of big wheels from the highway. He put his ear to it and listened for movement behind the surface.

The screen kissed his face with the sudden, sharp sound of a scream.

Martin knew it was the boy.

He reeled back against the children's slide as his leg collapsed. Now the numbness was going for his body. He hauled himself up and pounded steel with his fist.

Not this time, he thought.

The solid screen was held erect by a frame of support beams, with a covered storage area in back.

The door to the storage shed was falling off its hinges.

He entered, following the crossbars of the supporting scaffold. Stacked lumber teetered overhead and paint cans rattled when he kicked them.

He knew at once that he was not alone in the enclosed space.

"Chris?"

He heard a shuffling, ahead and a little to the left.

"Are you all right?"

Then nothing.

"Stay where you are . . ."

He bumped into a barricade of packing cartons. As they tipped over, something squealed and jumped at him. Then another and another, as an army of snarling cats ran the scaffold.

"Hold on. I'm coming . . ."

Yellow mirror eyes observed his progress. He heard the toothpick bones of rat skeletons crunching underfoot. As his vision expanded to take in more of the utility shed, he saw other, larger shapes.

"Talk to me, Chris!"

A scrape, then a sizzle, and a blue spark flared in an arc beyond the bars of the scaffold, blinding him.

Someone struck a match.

A few inches above the orange circle, a face was watching Martin, its features obscured by the glare of the flame.

The man's eyes, two tiny reflected flames, never left Martin's as he lit the butt of a cigar. He moved the wooden match away from his face, and as the end of the cigar glowed brighter Martin saw that Christopher was standing with him.

"Let him go," Martin said.

The man dropped the match and put his arm around Christopher's shoulders. Then he took the butt out of his mouth and tossed it.

From the corners, cats' eyes followed the trajectory to a puddle of water.

Now it was dark.

"I said, let the boy go."

Martin started forward, and bumped into the scaffold. A loose two-by-four rolled off the platform and thumped endfirst onto the ground.

The man laughed, a sound like wet thunder. Then he shook the scaffold with one hand. That was all it took.

The rest of the lumber rolled down like logs.

Martin felt the splintering impact, the crack of wood against bone and the searing coolness on his scalp when the wetness opened. He raised his hands to protect himself but they were now as cold as the place in his head where the night was rushing in. He was driven out through a hole in his skull, an opening so narrow he could not find his way back through the darkness. Down below, a part of him heard someone calling his name but the voice was too far away to help and then it was, it really was too late.

Lissa ran through tall grass. The blades parted before her, bowing to what was left of the sun on the horizon ahead. She came out of the field in time to see Will leave the gate and disappear along the fence.

Then there was a cry from inside the drive-in.

Will called, "Lissa!"

He had found a break in the fence, where it passed behind the screen.

He was on his hands and knees.

A section of chain links had been rolled up by vandals or determined animals. Lissa hooked her fingers through the links and pulled, hating her small hands. She straightened her back and bent the opening so that it was high enough for him to slide under.

Now there was a loud crash from a shed in back of the screen. The wooden support beams teetered as the screen resettled, loosing a cloud of dust to fog the sky.

"Wait," Will told her.

A breeze blew in off the ocean. She wrapped her arms around her thin sides. Beyond the salt flats, on the other side of the highway, a last blazing slice of sun hovered above the water. Behind her, a wave of darkness swept across the acres of marsh grass that separated her from the apartment complex.

After a minute she said, "Will?"

He did not answer.

Where had he gone?

The opening in the fence was only a few inches high. She stuffed her hair under her collar, lay down on her back and shimmied under. The steel links picked at the front of

117

her sweater. Once she was inside she kicked free and rolled over.

And saw eyes watching her. They were low to the ground and so round and wide that their pupils caught the red wavelengths of the refracted sunset. They did not blink.

She shifted to a crouching position.

When she tossed a stone the eyes withdrew. Then more eyes took their place, holding her in their reflective gaze, as a splintering sound came from inside the storage shed.

She got up and ran to it.

The door was hanging open. She entered the darkness with her arms held out, and heard a grunt. Then something huge rose up in front of her. She felt her shoe catch in the loose boards and could not step aside in time to avoid it. She locked her elbows to ward it off, as the shape brushed past her and stumbled outside.

She saw a tall, heavy figure outlined in the protracted twilight. Suddenly the top half disappeared, as though cut off at the waist.

When her eyes adjusted she recognized Will, stooping to lower Martin from a fireman's carry.

"Will, is he . . . ?"

She pressed her ear to Martin's chest.

118

There was the rushing of the sea beneath his ribs. She raised her head, inches from his chin, and saw past his lips to the running gash on the side of his skull.

Will moved Martin's head. "His neck's not broken."

"What happened?"

"I don't know." Will was breathing heavily. "It looks like a ton of shit fell on him."

"I'll get help," she said.

She went around to the front of the screen. There were the spidery shapes of the playground equipment. The swings creaked slowly. She looked across the lot to the snack bar, hoping to spot a pay phone, and realized that even if there was one it would be disconnected.

Now the swings flopped wildly. She saw a cat leap out of the sandbox and race away between the speaker posts. Others followed, pouring out of the shed and scattering to the four corners.

If there are cats here, she thought, there must be rats. Where? How many? She shuddered.

She returned to the break in the fence. She would have to go back across the marsh, to the apartments, to call for help. There was no choice.

"Christ," said Will, "where's the kid?"

"Oh God . . ."

"CHRIS!" he bellowed. "GET YOUR ASS OVER HERE!"

No answer.

A sound like the surf gathered force in her ears. She looked in the other direction. There were only flatlands and the line of the coast highway between here and the ocean. Not even a car in sight.

She got back under the fence, tearing her sweater open. Then the drive-in was at her back and she was running into the field of tall grass.

Follow the lights, she told herself.

It was no use trying to watch her step. The marsh was black underfoot. Flashes of water flew up around her, reeds bent and sprang back, then broke and fell away under the steady slap of her shoes. Soon her hair was dripping, her face scratched and muddy. When one of her low heels broke, she stopped long enough to get rid of her shoes.

In the grass ahead, someone cleared his throat.

She froze.

She heard water dripping, and a rustling as something slithered closer, encircling her. The stalks moved and then were still under a starless sky. A river of blood coursed in her ears. She held her breath and listened to the silence.

The throat began to croak.

It was a deep, woody sound, very close by. Other voices answered, and an entire chorus of bullfrogs took up the chant. Then there was the high trilling of crickets, as the marsh came alive to the night.

She took a deep breath and started moving again.

The reeds were too tall for her to see where she was going. The sky was the same slate-gray color in all directions. She spread the stalks immediately in front of her, only to find a denser layer beyond. Where were the lights? Somehow she had taken a wrong turn, and now she was lost. She cursed herself. It was absurd. The apartments were only a few hundred yards away.

Jack's hurt, she thought. He needs help. And the little boy, Christopher . . . She didn't want to think about that.

I have to keep going. It doesn't matter what happens to me, as long as I get there.

She chose a new direction and forced herself forward. Slime sucked at her toes, then sand and rocks, then something more slippery that wriggled when she stepped on it. She splashed ahead in what she thought was a straight line, as a pounding rhythm filled her ears.

This time it was not her heartbeat.

There were heavy, splashing feet in the field behind her. Someone else had entered the marshland and was coming this way, tearing down everything in his path.

She felt the panic then, pulsing in her temples and contracting her stomach. For a moment she thought of throwing up in an effort to purge the fear, but there was not time for that. She clawed at the reeds. They were thick here and deeply rooted. She hurled herself through, and fell face-first into a sparkling puddle.

The footsteps closed the distance. She heard them crushing the grass, hammering the ground. The wet skin of the earth trembled beneath her hands. She twisted around and threw her arms over her face as the stalks collapsed around her.

The pounding stopped.

She opened her eyes.

A tall, terrible figure stood over her.

It had two heads.

One of the heads opened its swollen mouth and tried to speak.

"Put me down . . ."

It was Jack.

"Sure?"

"Uh."

Will let Jack down from his back.

She stood up, pulling her torn sweater together over her chest.

"H-how did you get him under the fence?"

"Not under," said Will. She noticed his bleeding arms. "Over."

"My God . . ."

She saw past them down the long swath Will had cut through the grass. Beyond the drive-in the sky was not yet completely dark. The last traces of daylight still shone through a break in the fogbank. At the edge of the flatlands the coast highway was a narrow ribbon of liquid silver, unsteady as a mirage.

"Look!" she said.

There were two figures walking on the horizon.

A bus came into view from the north, its sides awash with the colors of the sunset through striated clouds. There was the distant hissing of air brakes as the bus stopped in front of an enormous, coruscating sun.

The two figures might have been a man and a boy. They waited for the doors to open.

Then the doors pumped shut and they were gone.

The bus moved on, smeared with red, as the sun submerged in a boiling firestorm.

6.

The rough hand was so much larger than his own that his fingers disappeared inside it along with his thumb and part of his wrist, a palm as thick and hard as the bark of a tree, clasping him tightly so that he felt only the pressure and the power that pulled him along. The hand lifted him with such force that his feet lost contact with the ground and skimmed along the blacktop in the way that a needle skates across the surface of a record. Then the rubber toes of his shoes were raking the metal steps, skipping along the aisle before setting down again on the sticky floor by the last row of seats. The engine rumbled and heavy tires rolled somewhere underneath him.

He held his neck rigid and did not look to

either side. The other seats were unoccupied, their steel frames jerking with each movement of the bus. The aisle was long, and very far away, at the other end, the driver's shoulders hunched as black gloves rode the huge steering wheel around the curve of the highway. It grew dark out and darker inside. The bus swayed, the horizon line bobbed up at the bottom of the windows, and then the windows were blank again. The hand that held his hand never let go.

Now, above the rumble of the engine and the rattle of the seats, he heard a hissing, popping crackle. A voice spoke from overhead:

"I need two tickets."

It was the driver, speaking from a perforated circle in the ceiling.

In the seat next to Christopher's, the tall man said nothing.

"Let me see your tickets or your money."

A truck passed, towing a half-section of a mobile home. Beyond the flapping edge of plastic sheeting, Christopher made out the shadow shapes of a living room, clean and perfect. The truck accelerated and the living room moved away from him.

"In the back. I'm talking to you."

The bus driver put on the air brakes and

pulled over to the side of the highway and glared into the mirror.

"Hey, man, are you deaf?"

The driver stood up, attempting to see his only passengers. He threw a switch and the overhead lights buzzed as if flies were trapped inside the panels, then flickered on.

He came down the aisle. His forehead was taut and he was not smiling. His face became larger until his bulging features filled Christopher's field of vision.

"No tickee," said the driver, "no ride. Understand?"

Christopher wanted to speak. It was too late for him. But it was not too late for the driver. If he could only warn him in time.

"You're not deaf, are you, boy? You understand me. I can see it in your eyes."

He extended his muscular arm to pat Christopher on the head, then turned his attention to the other seat.

"You got money, old man? Because if you don't, I got to—"

Before he could touch Christopher's hair, there was a clicking sound and a blade flicked through the air, the point stopping an inch from the driver's belt. The tip was aimed directly at his crotch.

127

The vein at his temple pulsed, ticking off the seconds as cars passed, rocking the bus.

Finally the driver said, "Sometimes it ain't worth it, you know?"

The blade disappeared with a click.

The driver remembered to breathe.

"You got yourself a free ride. To the end of the line."

After a while they were moving again. Still Christopher did not turn his head. He knew what he would see there next to him, and he did not want to look into its eyes.

The rocking lulled him. He wanted to go to sleep and wake up from this dream, could not, and so the rhythm of the bus took over and there was nothing else. The grinding of gears, the squeaking of seats, the sloshing of the toilet behind the door and the motion of tires on the rise and fall of the highway were all there was for him.

At some point a new sound entered the dream. There was a voice outside. It bleated insistently and would not go away. The voice got louder as it paced them on the left, fell back and tried to pass on the right. Christopher felt the engine straining as the bus driver floored the accelerator. Then the horn outside was a steady blare. He kept his eyes closed and waited for it to stop. He heard the beat of a muffler and pistons screaming at full throttle as the car made one more try to get ahead of them, drew even with the bus, and tapped the steel side with its fender. Tires screeched and Christopher tumbled forward as the bus cut its speed. He put his hands out, but then brakes locked and only the raised headrest on the back of the next seat prevented him from flying into the aisle.

When he came to, the noise was over. A hot spot burned on his forehead and he thought he was still moving. The water in the toilet splashed like an ocean in a bottle, slowing. He opened his eyes and saw that the bus had stopped, nosed down at an angle on the side of the road. How long had it been this way? He remembered the man letting go of his hand, the weight moving over him to the aisle, and then nothing. Now he felt the man back in the seat, the shoulder against his. He drew away from the hardness of it, as cold and heavy as a bag of cement.

Far ahead, the driver was not at the wheel under the buzzing, flickering lights. Had he hit his head, too, and fallen to the floor? There was no crack in the windshield.

Christopher heard an animal scratching at the front door of the bus.

The flaps rippled but the door would not open. Then there was a crunching impact and one of the safety glass panels in the door collapsed inward, rounded pieces falling like bits of sticky candy. Christopher saw a hand that held a tire iron reach inside and release the manual lever, and a man climbed aboard. The lights were flickering on and off and the face was a shadow lit by lightning.

The man started down the aisle, iron bar in hand.

Christopher tried to remember a house and hot food and a bed with blankets and his mother to smooth the knot from his fore-head. He could not hold the thought because the man in the aisle was speaking.

"Chris."

He knew that voice.

"Chris, come with me."

He moved a fraction of an inch. Next to him, the weight leaned harder on his arm but there was no longer a hand holding his.

He took a chance and leaped out of the seat.

As he pressed his body against Will, the

130

man in the other seat began sliding to the floor.

Will reached around Christopher and grabbed the man by the lapels, hauling him up.

"*Who are you?* What do you—?"

Christopher dared to look at the other passenger's face for the first time.

It was not the tall man.

It was the driver, his black-gloved hands limp on the ends of his arms. His head was down. And something was wrong with his neck. Were those bubbles under his chin?

"What the hell . . . ?"

Then, though the bus did not move, there was a sloshing from the toilet behind the door.

Will let go of the driver and raised the tire iron.

With his other hand he took hold of the door lever.

Before he could open it, the door swung wide.

The shadow inside grew like an inflating doll till it was so tall it almost touched the ceiling. Then it was in the aisle, so fast that Christopher could not even try to warn Will, because the knife was out and the tall man was upon them.

131

"Can't you go any faster?"

"Easy, ma'am. We'll get there."

Ma'am, thought Lissa. Who does he think I am, his mother?

She watched the young, crewcut officer drive effortlessly through the fog. His hands rested on the wheel at the ten-and-two positions, textbook perfect, the dainty clock-springs of golden hair on his knuckles dyed green by the light from the instrument panel. The long barrel of a shotgun rose vertically between them, held erect by a lock on the dashboard. The speedometer remained as steady on the curves as on the straightaway, regardless of visibility. He knew the road and drove it by rote and nothing would change his routine.

"How much farther?"

He took several seconds to respond, as though he had to translate her words into another language and check them against a list of approved answers before replying.

"At the turnoff."

"Which one?"

"Old Oak Road. It's about five miles outside of Shadow Bay."

"I know where it is."

They took the curve and his foot did not lift on the gas pedal despite the blowing fogbank. The headlights in the southbound lane were creeping so slowly, hugging the rail, that the cars might have been standing still. There was something to be said for consistency. . . .

She had called an ambulance for Jack and, when Will did not return, the police. It took the young officer only a few minutes to get to her apartment, but he made her tell him everything that had happened before allowing her into the ambulance with Jack. As she was climbing in with the paramedics, a call came through on the police radio. They had found the bus. She got out of the ambulance, placed herself in front of the squad car and refused to move unless he took her with him.

"Warm enough for you?"

"What?"

"The heater. I can turn it down."

"No. Please."

She put her hands closer to the vent. The airflow felt like warm water on her skin, though the small bones in her fingers remained cold.

He was more accommodating when asking the questions. That was what he had been trained for. When she asked him something he withdrew behind a defensive shield, so as not to relinquish control. To protect and to serve, she thought. And to dominate. She suspected that he had his own reasons for allowing her to go along. For identification? The idea made her sick to her stomach. What if I asked him to stop the car so I can throw up? Would he do it? Probably not. I'll bet he has a traffic sickness bag in the glove compartment. Official issue. Leaving nothing to chance. Always prepared, like an overgrown Boy Scout.

A sign whipped by in the fog:

OLD OAK RD. 500 FEET

"Here," she said.

He did not slow. He handled his CB microphone and spoke a few words in a kind of techno-military jargon she did not understand, as their high beams glanced off a solid wall of mist. With the whiteness all around there was no sensation of movement, only the revs of the engine and the occasional rock or bit of gravel hitting the underside of the car. Then one, two, three pink circles, fuzzy stains surrounded by halos, came up in front of them. The circles bled larger, turning from pink to red and Lissa saw that they were revolving lights on top of three police cars. Hats and fur collars crossed between the cars and the silver side of a Greyhound bus that had run into a ditch. The officer set the parking brake, leaving the engine and headlights on.

She got out and ran to the front of the bus. "Where's the car?"

"What car?" said one of the policemen, a Sheriff's Deputy from Santa Mara.

"I thought you found his—" His what? She did not know what kind of car Will drove. The young officer had said they'd found it. Hadn't he?

"Stand aside," said the Deputy.

Another red light broke through the fog. This one was an ambulance. The Deputy took her elbow and led her off the road. The young officer scraped a flare on the pavement as though striking a match and set it out on the center line, where it hissed on its side like a defective Roman candle. The Deputy directed the ambulance crew to the bus.

She slipped ahead of them and climbed on board. Glass pebbles crunched under her shoes. The aisle was a dark tunnel. Then an ambulance attendant came up behind her with a flashlight.

135

"In back," someone said.

Her eyes followed the beam. All the seats were empty, except for the last row, against the rear wall.

"Miss," said the attendant, "please . . ."

As flashlights converged, she saw a man propped up with his head down, his hands clamped between his knees and his elbows locked at an unnatural angle.

The driver's uniform was covered with a dark wetness. When someone lifted his chin his throat opened and more blood dribbled out of his slashed throat.

There was no one else on the bus.

There are varieties of fear.

The first is unease, a sense that all may not be as it appears. This is the feeling you have when you know something is wrong but you don't know what it is yet.

Then there is anxiety, a warning that it might be better not to know what is out there. This is the one that makes you call in sick instead of going to work, with no excuse that anyone would understand.

Next comes the apprehension that wakes

you in the night and says, For God's sake don't turn on the light! It breathes on your neck in the dark and you know it has to be more than your imagination, because *something* is there.

Finally there is the panic that means someone is about to break your door down and there is nothing you can do about it. This is a primitive reaction that leaves you beating your chest and howling at the moon, ready to kill or be killed, and by then it is too late for any kind of reason.

But stronger than any of these is what the rabbit feels an instant before the club falls: total systemic shutdown, with respiration suspended and heart stopped, a simulation of death that is the only chance for survival. It is a kind of death in life, past instinct or reflex, thought or desire. Beyond it there is nothing but the void.

That is the way it was for Christopher.

He sat in the front seat of the Mustang, between two bodies. His legs were too short to reach the floor; under the light from the instruments his knees glowed through the holes in his jeans like radioactive faces. The interior smelled of rusty metal and damp fabric and clotted blood. The bodies moved from time to time as the car swung around a

137

curve, drifting over the center line, and the one on his right slid against him, about to keel over into his lap. Then headlights hit the windshield and a horn smeared past. The one who was driving turned the wheel and the other body flopped away, and for a moment Christopher could breathe again.

Where are we going? he wondered.

Not far, a voice answered.

But where?

To Box City.

The sound was not in the car. There was the hawking of the muffler, the squeaking of the seats, the ticking of the clock on the dashboard. The sound came from inside him, where the fear lived.

Why are we going there?

Because it is safe.

Safe from what?

From those who would hurt you.

But YOU want to hurt me!

Never.

The car swerved up an inclined road. Christopher's body became heavier. He heard the sound of tires like rain under the car, the thudding of Will's skull against the headliner. Ahead, the high beams swept dead oak trees. A branch clawed at the top of the car. A jackrabbit pretended to be a statue, its eyes red as if filling with blood.

Then let me go.

That is what they want.

Why?

To keep us apart.

Who are they?

Try to forget . . .

The road leveled. The front tires swung out into space, found the dirt again. Outside the windshield there was only blackness now, blackness and stars.

Am I going to die?

Yes.

Now?

Not yet.

When?

All things must die. It is not yours to know.

The car wound around the hillside and began to descend. The fog blew away and the lights of the town below were stars gone to earth and he felt that he was falling up. Finally the car yawed to a stop. Far away, streets were laid out in a grid dotted with lampposts. Above the car trees rustled on the cliffs.

Open the door.

Please . . .

Do it.

No . . .

Now.

I can't!

The man got out. When he opened the door the wind blew through. He pulled Christopher after him. Then he moved the body over behind the wheel.

He was my friend.

You don't have any friends.

I did.

I am your only friend.

The man released the brake and the Mustang rolled down into a ravine. In the gaping darkness below, branches snapped and wild dogs began to bark.

Now there is no one to keep you from me.

They walked down a white path. The mist rose, swirled up to the trees and hung in the leaves, as if parting before them. Somewhere close by, black water ran past to the sea.

Are you afraid?

Yes.

Don't be. I am with you.

As the mist lifted from the ground, the boy's feet disappeared in darkness, cut off at the ankles. The dark concealed other things, too. He heard night animals scratching at the stones and shagging up trees, hastening to fresh hiding places. Then the ground ahead opened and larger eyes were watching them.

They won't bother us.

How do you know?

They are the Box People.

There were other feet behind, following, closing in. The boy did not look back.

The path led to a clearing, a circle of cardboard boxes that had sagged and melted in the falling dampness. A short distance past the boxes were wooden crates big enough to hold TV sets or refrigerators. One of the crates wobbled and opened, and a man greeted them.

"Welcome, brothers," he said. He was thin, his hair tied in a ponytail. "Do you know the Articles?"

They walked on.

The thin man kept up with them.

"We can talk about it in the morning. If you need a place to sleep . . ."

Another path led down from the far side of the clearing. Below, a dark crater yawned wide. A smell worse than the red tide drifted up. Christopher drew back.

141

The thin man took the boy's other hand.

"I'll show you the way."

Click.

The knife point made an arc, like a falling star.

"Hey, no need for violence, brother."

The thin man let go, backing to the edge of the crater. He craned his neck to see who he was talking to.

He saw.

"Forget I said anything. I didn't know . . ."

Click.

They went down without him.

The stink got stronger and the ground was soft and crunchy. They skirted half-buried bedsprings, plastic bottles, trash bags full of curdled jelly. Then the tops of funny little houses broke through the mist. They were made of rough metal and there was a warm glow between the cracks in one of them.

Inside, someone stirred. What would have been a door shuddered open and an old man leaned out. Within the rude shack a candle guttered over a lumpy mattress surrounded by stacks of books.

"Please, I'm trying to work. My office hours are . . ."

He shone a flashlight in their faces, the filament twitching like a dying firefly behind the cracked lens. Then he lowered the flashlight, his chin quivering.

"I didn't know it was you," he said.

He left the shack.

Minutes later Christopher was lying on the mattress, the candle snuffed out, the tall man next to him. They lay side by side in the fetid darkness.

Sleep.

Yes . . .

Tomorrow, I will take you to the city.

The boy saw meaningless patterns on the low ceiling. He was in a boat tossing on the stinking waves. A ship with a searchlight drew alongside and threw a life rope. His arms were too short to catch it, so the ship extinguished its light and sailed on. He remained where he was, the water lapping closer, sloshing into his boat. After a while his eyes closed. He heard a breathing that was not his own in the narrow room, and the clicking of a knife as it opened and shut, opened and shut through the long night.

Part Three

Something White

7.

Why would you ask me a thing like that?

Dr. Underwood's office looked like a cheap hotel room, with a framed poster hanging on the wood-grain panels, a desk and unmatched chairs, and a faded, worn carpet that buckled where it met the wall. When is he going to finish moving in? she wondered. How long has it been, six years?

"Did you hear what I said, Miss Shelby?"

"I'm not sure I understand the question."

The psychiatrist leaned back, his large hands clasped behind his head. "I asked what it is you're afraid of."

Don't you work here, too? she thought. Don't you have eyes?

"Have you read my report?"

147

"Yes." He tipped back in his chair. His skull made contact with the picture frame, driving thick wrinkles across the top of his bald head. "Is there anything else?"

"It's all there," she said, indicating the report she had typed this morning, before work. Somehow he had replaced the paper clip in exactly the same position; the pages were squared up perfectly on his blotter, as if the topsheet had not been lifted at all.

"Are you sure?"

"I covered the important points, at least in summary. The behavioral changes, the withdrawal, the night terrors—"

"Why haven't I heard this from other staff?"

"I don't know," she said impatiently. "Why don't you ask them?"

"I will. If you give me something more to go on."

He doesn't believe me. Why should I need to argue the obvious? If he were doing his job, we wouldn't be having this conversation. We'd be busy planning a way to help these kids. That's our responsibility, isn't it?

A bell rang, signaling the end of first breakfast. Beyond the closed door, in the hall outside the office, children shuffled past on their way to the dayroom. There was no running, very little talking and no laughter. Didn't he have ears?

"I'm surprised no one else has spoken to you. Fitz knows." She groped for another name. "So does Bill Soon. In fact, just about everyone knows what's going on, I'm sure of it."

Underwood refused to meet her eyes and instead stared at the ceiling. Flecks of mica glittered there, embedded in the acoustic stucco; it reminded her of the ceiling in her apartment, where false stars shone overhead when she tried to sleep.

She heard one last pair of shoes enter the long hallway, moving at a slow, deliberate pace. Someone else was coming this way.

"What shift are you working now?"

The question took her by surprise. "Ten-to-six. Why?"

"Then you don't personally monitor Tiger Cottage at night."

"Lions," she corrected. "I have the split shift every third week, two-to-ten. The last time I had to set up bedding next to the office, because the Infirmary was full. The youngest ones wouldn't sleep in their rooms."

"Too many mice in the cage?"

"Pardon?"

"When the population is high, and they have to double up, there are bound to be problems. . . ."

"About the population," she said. "I've talked to Santa Mara and San Luis Obispo. It's not like this anywhere else."

"I haven't seen the figures . . ."

"Well, I have. And they're almost all runaways. I think we've got an epidemic on our hands, Doctor."

"What do you mean?" He frowned.

She sought the right word. "Call it fear."

"And what do you think is the cause of this fear?"

"For one thing, there was the child they found murdered last summer. Then the one on the beach Friday. And now the body over the weekend, in town." She decided not to mention what had happened Saturday night, at least not yet.

"I'm not sure I get your point." His head moved the landscape poster on the wall, tipping it several degrees out of kilter.

"The children know, don't you see? The little ones have known for a long time what's going on."

"Wait. The drowning—you called it a murder. That hasn't been determined yet, has it?"

"It doesn't matter. The point is that children are dying. My theory is that there may have been others, more than we've heard about. The children of Shadow Bay know something, but no one is paying attention. I think we'd better start listening to them before it's too late."

The footsteps in the hall grew louder as the landscape tilted more severely, straining against the nail in the wall.

"How much vacation time do you have, Lissa?"

"What?"

"It must be quite a lot by now, with all the overtime."

"What overtime?"

"You've been coming in weekends, haven't you?"

She had known to expect this. She held her eyes down, seeing her hands, pale and small and useless in her lap. "If you mean Saturday, that wasn't official. I came by to check the records." So I'd be prepared for this meeting. "May I ask you something?" she said quietly. "How many more are there like Ruthie J.?"

His head tapped the glass in the picture frame. If he was not careful it would break. He smiled peculiarly. "I appreciate your interest, but you can leave that part to me. Don't worry yourself about it."

If I don't, she thought, then who? Not you, apparently.

"Take some time off," Underwood continued. "Starting now, today. Get away from the Hall, go somewhere warm and sunny, and relax. We'll talk more about this when you get back."

Her jaw dropped open and touched her collar. Then she closed her mouth and bit down hard to keep her lips from quivering. She didn't want to give him that much. I'm intruding on his territory, she thought. It won't look good for him if I move on this before he does. It's as simple as that.

"I don't need a vacation," she said.

"You'll be surprised at the difference it can make."

"No, thank you."

"I'll talk to your supervisor. You've been under a lot of stress. Over-identification can lead to burnout. It happens to the best of us."

I'm stressed, you're stressed, we're all stressed. So what? The children need us to be here for them, now more than ever. Vacation? What is he talking about? Does he think I'm that weak?

She looked at her hands again. They were

stressed, too, clutching at her knees through her dress, wrinkling the fabric. And what about him? He was smug and placid behind his desk, the detached professional. Nothing ever gets to you, does it, Doctor, despite all the pain and suffering. What will it take? Screaming children, blood seeping under the door? Another body? A hundred? Give it time; it can be arranged. It won't be long now. It will be here soon.

She said, "I understand how it must seem to you. You only know what filters through this office. If you saw one disturbed child last week, then as far as you're concerned there aren't any others. That's the scientific method. Only . . . what if there really is something out there? If you can't see it, then what? What happens to the children?" Her fingers were cold, trembling. She pulled down the hem of her dress and shifted her legs to one side, preparing to stand. "I thought you'd want to help me in this, but now . . . I think I'd better go."

He smiled patronizingly, as if her words were not, could not have been intended for him.

"Is there anything else you want to tell me?"

153

"What more do you need?" She stood. "I'm sorry. I have to get back to work."

He was right. There was something else. But if she told him about Jack, the boy, Will . . . no, it would only confuse the issue.

"Something more than a hunch, than feelings," said the doctor. His tone was almost kind, his face almost cruel. "Otherwise, I'm afraid . . ."

The landscape behind his head changed then. It had been a generic forest scene. Now she noticed a dark shape between the trees, silhouetted at the end of a birchwood path. The shape was two-legged, with abnormally long arms. A bear? No, it was a man. A tall, terrible man whose face she could not see. He was coming this way.

"Can't you do something about that?" she snapped.

"Hmm?"

That. It was not a picture anymore. As she watched it the frame bent and expanded, the wood bowing, the path extending beyond the plane of the wall.

He swiveled in his chair, considered the landscape and turned back to her with a puzzled expression.

The shape moved out of the frame and

154

over the wall like an inkblot, to form a black halo behind the doctor's head.

"Stop it, please!"

"Sit down, Lissa." Underwood punched the intercom on his desk. "Code yellow," he said calmly.

She grabbed the coffee mug and hurled it. He ducked. It missed his head and struck the poster, shattering the glass. Sharp pieces rained down around him, as the frame opened wide. *It was the whole wall.*

Two attendants came through the door.

"Take Miss Shelby to the Infirmary," Underwood told them. "Ten cc's of diazepam . . ."

They were too busy strapping the jacket around her body to notice the way the blackness spread out and darkened the room. The metal bookcase sagged under the weight of it; in the corner the file cabinet rocked from side to side and began chattering forward. She felt her hands drawn across her chest and up under her armpits. She tried to fight the attendants but her arms were weak in the canvas. She arched her back and kicked the desk over. As the lights went out completely she saw again the meaningless pattern on the ceiling—

And sat up.

Above her, the ceiling of her bedroom flickered in the morning light.

She hugged her pillow. The slipcase was damp. When she looked up, the rising sun beamed through the cloud cover outside, penetrating the curtains and illuminating the curled edges of one of the papers on her wall. It was a yellowed painting by Marcie, a heart with oversized lettering:

STAY
CLOSE
TO
ME

She buried her face in the pillow and wept.

I shouldn't have let that cop at the hospital bully me, she thought. I should have stayed with Jack, just to be there with him, and not gone home no matter what.

She stretched the phone cord to the balcony and gazed blearily outside. The empty stone paths between the apartments glistened with a silver webbing of dew. There was no evidence of life in any window; cur-

tains were still drawn and shades remained
down. For an instant she wondered if she
were the only one alive within the walled
community. Then she noticed a cat—was it
Idi?—under the acacia tree. It was dragging
something dark and wet. There was a furious
thrashing amid dead leaves. Then the mulch
settled and all was quiet again. As she looked
down, the dove-gray overcast foreshortened
the perspective so that the complex appeared
flat, two-dimensional. She shook her head
and turned to the marshlands beyond the
wall for some sense of scale. The drive-in
stood alone on the horizon, odd and useless,
like a tattered fairground after the circus has
moved on. The police had searched it last
night, found nothing but makeshift living
quarters in the shed behind the screen,
where the homeless nested. Even here, she
thought, so close. I never noticed.

"Hello?"

"I'm still here."

"Mr. Martin is doing much better."

"Can you put me through?"

"I'm sorry, there's no answer."

"I'll come get him, then."

"Not just yet."

"Why not?"

"The doctor wants to run some tests."

"How long will that take?"

"I couldn't say. We'll call you as soon as we have the results."

"I'm coming over."

"Really, Mrs. Martin, there's no need—"

"I'm not Mrs. Martin."

"Then who—?"

Lissa broke the connection.

She was afraid again. She remembered the tall, dark, terrible figure moving across the flatlands to the highway. The smaller figure climbing aboard the bus with him, their hands linked, before the steel door shut. Then Will taking off in his car to chase them. What they found on the bus later. And what they didn't find.

She felt a tingling in her spine, creeping along the back of her neck and then to her scalp, as if someone had come up behind her and now stood only inches away, ready to touch her.

She glanced in at her living room one last time. The gray light slanting through the sliding glass balcony doors softened the folds of the blanket on the floor, the edges of the sofa, the TV set on its cart and the mug on the coffee table. For a moment it was hard for her to believe that anyone lived in the apartment. Now it seemed as insubstantial as a movie set, an oil-smoked interior waiting to be struck as soon as she left. Would it be here when she came back? She was not sure that she wanted it to be. The TV screen reflected the room in its convex eye, a collection of props too hopelessly cluttered for habitation. She closed the door on the distorted jumble and keyed the deadbolt, wondering if she would ever find the time and strength to put it all in order.

Mist clung to the rails, heavy as melting paint, as she descended the cement steps. Splotches of moisture darkened the walkway, as if an unknown visitor had traversed the complex during the night, leaving a wet trail along every connecting path, dripping puddles by every door. The trees were silent and unmoving, pendulous with water. Somewhere within the labyrinth of buildings a baby cried and would not stop. Lissa stretched the neck of her sweater up over her chin and hurried on to the underground garage.

I'll talk to Jack first, she thought, and get our stories straight, before the police ask me anything else. It will sound crazy. The Man With No Face. And a little boy who doesn't exist, according to the system. And what about Will? They didn't even find his car. Is anybody going to listen?

The stairway to the garage was dim and indistinct. As she descended she stepped over puddles until they became too large and formless to avoid. It was as if the porous walls bled perpetually, never allowing the cement to dry out. The skins of the parked cars ran with condensation, their once-bright colors hazy and blanched. The landau top of a Ford Crown Victoria was spackled with a white mineral crust, the luggage rack on the roof of a Volvo station wagon released corrosive teardrops onto the laminate door panels. Swollen radial tires bulged like fat black snakes under the wheel wells of dented fenders, sidewalls cracking and rubber treads rotting into pools of liquefaction. When Lissa got to her row she began to walk faster, splashing icy water over her ankles.

She came to the end of the row and stopped, key in hand.

There was her Datsun, nosed inconspicuously to the wall, with its oxidized paint and the rusty hole in the trunk where the lock had been drilled out before she bought it.

It was her car, and yet it was not. It couldn't be. She saw the familiar fingermarks on her windows, the old nicks and scratches and the crease in the bumper, the battered license plate with the same number. But the car was narrower than she remembered, slewed across into the next space, where it rested in an unnatural alignment.

She walked around to the driver's side.

And saw that the side of her car was smashed, the door deeply damaged and the safety glass spidered with cracks. There was no other car nearby. There never was. That was why she had made this her spot. Nonetheless one side of her car was caved in, as if it had been sideswiped, struck by a powerful and invisible force during the night.

The gulls settled over the shack.

Christopher heard them touch down, wings beating, claws scoring the corrugated roof, their beaks tapping out a code. He lay on his back and wondered what they were saying.

It's time.

Not yet, he thought.

Yes.

Please . . .

Now.

He focused his eyes around grains of sleep. Shadows feathered the torn curtains as more gulls swooped low.

He heard springs releasing inside the old mattress, heavy shoes shaking the floor. Then the door banged open at the end of the bed and the bad smell blew in. The tall man had his back to him so even in the morning light he could not see the face. Gulls cawed across the doorway.

Christopher got up and followed the man out.

Other shacks like this one surrounded a bumpy plain at the bottom of a crater. Gulls flew over the plain, searching the debris. Now a small tribe of men and women had come out and were busy digging up pieces of metal and plastic to fortify their own shacks. There were children, too. Christopher heard them shout and giggle as they chased the gulls, waving their hands and pumping their short legs.

Next to him, the tall man raised the collar of his overcoat around the sides of his face.

One gull broke away and left the flock. It

flew close with beak open and beady eyes fixed, hovering in front of Christopher, riding the currents up and down.

It's hungry, he thought.

Yes.

Can we feed it?

It must learn to survive.

Oh, please?

Christopher moved his arm over his head and the gull dropped closer.

The tall man took the boy's hand. His other hand shot out and caught the bird as if plucking an apple out of the air. The gull flapped and pecked as the man examined it.

Are you hungry?

Yes, but . . .

Its heart is strong and its blood is warm. It will nourish us. Take out your knife.

No!

Then I will show you how, this time.

Don't . . .

The man let go of Christopher's hand and petted the bird to calm it. Then he closed his fingers around its neck. It happened too quickly for the bird to protest. One second it was looking at the man's thumb. Then there was a snap and the bird's head fell to the side and its wings were flapping again. Then the click of a blade and the head was on the

163

ground, the arrow tongue scooping dirt. Blood showered down.

Eat.

I won't!

Blood continued to rain over his head but the boy kept his mouth closed, holding his chin to his chest.

You will be hungrier, later.

I don't care!

In the distance, other birds caught the scent and rose up in a cloud.

The women stopped what they were doing. When they saw, they called their children to them.

As the tall man led Christopher out of the camp, no one spoke. The men and women hung back, standing very still. Their eyes were even more alert than the eyes of the gulls that watched from above, on the rim of the crater.

Did you sleep?

Christopher did not answer.

Try to forget the nightmare.

You know about that?

It was only a dream, as are we all.

8.

Leanne threw her legs over the side of the bed.

As she poked around for her slippers, her toes touched the naked floor . . .

She felt a cold shock.

And drew back, her foot curling involuntarily.

She unsealed her eyes and peeped over the edge.

There were the slippers, the fur-lined ones that had been Jack's, on the braided rug by the bed. How had she managed to touch the floor? She would have had to stretch her leg all the way to the spot where the rug ended and the boards began. Too far to reach.

I must have been dreaming, she thought.

She rose on her elbow and tried again,

more cautiously this time. There were her toes, the third longer than the second, the little one a flattened nub clinging to its neighbor, the nails pinched half-moon wedges, hard and cracked. How ugly! She lowered her foot . . .

And jerked it away.

The slipper felt nasty, wet.

That was not possible.

Then an image strobed before her, painted on the air:

A long, narrow body with an insectoid head on an impossibly thin neck, snapping at her foot. The head was made of slotted steel, like the speaker box you hook on your window at a drive-in movie. The neck reached its maximum extension and the head stopped short and swung away, bumping her shin and tearing out a divot of flesh.

She dragged her foot back under the covers and rubbed her leg.

The skin was smooth, untouched.

The air cleared, and the image was gone.

A memory?

She and Jack had gone to a drive-in movie down the coast a few times that first summer, what was it called? But nothing like this had ever happened, she was sure.

She thought, I'm getting sick. Ever since Friday night. I need more sleep . . .

The phone rang.

This was not the first time. It had rung again and again through the night and into the early morning.

Damn you, Steve, grow up!

He had a way of pushing, pushing and never backing off long enough to give her a chance to breathe. Well, this time it wouldn't work. She did not feel sadness or even disappointment. For once she felt nothing. She would not even turn on the answering machine to give him the satisfaction of hearing her voice.

After ten or twelve rings, he gave up.

She covered her face with the flannel sheet. Now, under her tent, she listened to the seagulls talking on her roof, the plash of the tide, the raspy electric babble of a TV cartoon show from the next house, the jingle of a shopping cart negotiating the curb at the end of the block. No children? Then she remembered. The murder . . . was that it? Were their parents too afraid to let them out of the house even on Sunday morning? Unless they catch him, whoever he is, she thought, I won't ever see or hear any of them again. For now, the gulls walked the tar-

167

paper roof, pecking gravel as if it were bird-seed, their talons ready to penetrate the cracks between the boards in her ceiling.

She lowered the tent and sat up, shook out a cigarette from the night table, lit it, took a drag, coughed and stubbed it out.

Maybe I'll stay in bed all day, she thought. What if Steve comes over? He has a key . . . I'll stick a chair under the back door-knob. Or the kitchen table, turn it on its side. What about the front door? I could pretend I'm not home, hide under the covers, not moving a muscle, or under the bed, or in the closet. If he finds me, I'll pretend I'm dead.

What if that turns him on?

The phone rang again.

All right, dammit, this is it!

She crawled off the bed and padded to the living room. She snatched up the receiver, digging her fingernails into the plastic.

"All right, Steve, I've had it!"

She hung up.

That ought to hold him, she thought.

She went to the kitchen, rinsed out her cup, filled it with bottled water, stuck it in the microwave, reached for the apricot tea in the cupboard. Her fingers touched the bottle of Orendain tequila Jack had brought from Mexico . . .

At that moment she heard gears clashing outside, as a truck passed her house.

She looked out the kitchen window and saw only the house next door, the empty alley.

She measured the tea and put it back. As she moved the bottle out of the way and closed the cupboard, she heard the screak of worn brake drums. It reminded her of broken chalk on a blackboard.

She started the timer on the microwave with a shaky finger.

Her feet were cold, so cold . . .

She left the kitchen to get her socks.

Halfway across the living room, she heard the brakes again, louder and closer. A truck? It sounded like a moving van, one of those block-long rigs with dozens of wheels.

She opened the curtains.

It wasn't a truck. It was a Greyhound bus, the sides dull as fogged mirrors, the tinted windows so dark that she could not see the passengers. The bus shuddered past her house like a ship coming into harbor, the enormous balloon tires scraping the curb, lacerating the sidewalls.

Wait a minute, she thought.

What is a bus doing in front of my house?

169

They never come this way. This is a dead-end street.

It rolled to the end of the block, to the intersection with the bike path.

He must be lost.

The microwave timer *ding*ed in the kitchen, a single note, clear and crystalline as a meditation bell.

She turned from the window as if waking.

While the tea steeped, she went for her socks, and then into the bathroom.

She flushed the toilet and brushed her teeth and picked up the water glass by the basin. HUSSONG'S, read the lettering. It was one of the set Jack had bought in Ensenada . . .

As she touched it to her lips, a trickle of blood ran from her mouth. The drops hit the wet porcelain like exploding stars. The glass, she thought, it's broken! How badly was she cut? She slammed the medicine cabinet to see the mirror. The rotted frame splintered under the impact. The mirror dropped out, carrying her image with it. The water glass slipped through her fingers as she stepped back.

She knew what would happen now.

Her calves met the tub and she lost her balance. Then her fingers closed on the shower curtain. It tore loose with a series of pops and she fell backward. She held on to the sink as the mirror broke into shards. One long piece flipped over the edge and jack-knifed into the carpet, an inch from her foot. She managed to right herself as more falling glass cut into her knuckles . . .

The phone rang.

She hobbled to the living room, on the verge of hysteria.

"Steve, I need you!" she said into the phone. She bunched up her nightgown and squeezed it to stop the bleeding in her hand. "I'm—"

"Mrs. Martin?"

"Who?"

"Mrs. Leanne Martin?"

"I—I'm sorry, I can't—"

"Is your husband John William Martin?"

"Yes. I mean—"

At the end of the block, the bus attempted to navigate the corner, an elephant trying to turn around in a phone booth. Where was it going? It wouldn't fit on the bike path. Even with the front wheels cut sharply it ran over the curb and clipped the guardrail, continuing for a full 180 degrees until it was facing back up her street.

"Mrs. Martin, I'm sorry to wake you, but—"

"Excuse me, can you talk a little louder?"

A flash of diffused sunlight swiped across the front windshield as it lined up with her house. A plume of black diesel smoke rose from the tail.

"This is the Santa Mara Sheriff's Department. We're calling about your husband."

She registered disbelief, then irritation, then resentment. Why call here? He wasn't her liability anymore. Yet she felt her lungs tightening and the cold ache opening in her chest. It was starting again.

The bus gunned its engine and rolled forward, picking up speed. It hit the curb in front of her house—it wasn't even trying to stay on the street. It was out of control. Was the driver drunk? No, not out of control . . .

He was aiming directly at her.

"I'm afraid there's been an accident . . ."

"For God's sake, *make it stop*!"

The bus crushed her fence, ripped into her lawn and charged her front window. Glass erupted and beams collapsed. The bus kept coming. Curtains spun round on the wheels, a cane rocker broke into matchsticks, the ceiling exploded and fell around her. The bus tore through the kitchen wall before the floor gave way and it nosed into the yawning core of the earth.

White-hot pain seared her leg. As rubble rained around her she saw that a wheel had passed over her toes, mashing them into pulp on the broken floorboards. Her sock bloomed red.

"Mrs. Martin, are you . . . ?"

She swayed against an intact wall for support. Were her toes still attached?

She opened her eyes, saw her feet and flexed her toes. They squirmed like fleshy worms inside her socks.

The pain stopped.

The roof was back. So was her bay window. The house was as it had always been, undamaged.

There was no bus.

There never had been.

The street outside was clear. A gull shaped like the top of a valentine winged away toward the horizon.

Her hand was cut, very slightly—that much was true. But not her lip.

She retraced the bloodstains to the bathroom.

The mirror was broken, as she knew it would be. She had seen it happen once before, on Friday night.

173

And what about the rest of it?

She had touched the slippers, the tequila bottle, the Mexican drinking glass . . . She had touched them, and she had seen.

They had all belonged to Jack.

She returned to the phone.

"Mrs. Martin, can you hear me? Your husband is at the Shadow Bay Medical Arts Center, near . . ."

I have to warn him, she thought.

Unless these things have happened to him already.

"I'll be right there."

Martin had no appetite.

The poached eggs, two floating white mounds, jiggled as he pushed the plate away.

The morning light hurt his eyes. It glared down mercilessly from the hospital window like an arctic sun through ice. He lifted the sketchpad from his lap long enough to move onto his side so that the window was at his shoulder. His right leg had fallen asleep again; pins and needles tingled in his veins from hip to toes. He was almost getting used to the feeling.

From this angle the eggs resembled breasts, the plate describing what might have been a rounded torso. He repositioned his knife and fork to represent legs, and dropped a tuft of parsley between them. Where was the head? Disgusted, he pushed the tray farther away from the bed.

There was a clattering in the hall as the door opened. A nurse pulled a cart to the middle of the room and began removing his breakfast.

"Something wrong with the food?"

Martin twisted around and forced himself to look outside.

"If you don't like eggs, I can bring you something else."

"Just black coffee."

"No coffee. Juice."

Martin fished in the bedclothes for his pen. He took up the Pilot Fineliner, tested the point and resumed drawing, this time on the napkin.

"If you drink your juice," said the nurse, "I might be able to find you some decaf."

He touched the pen to the cloth and held it there. As it took the ink, a cloudy shape flowed out and formed on the linen. It was a good medium, as snow-white as Bristol board and much more absorbent. He particularly liked the soft lines. He outlined the form and blacked it in, then sketched more of the amoeba-like shape. The napkin was hard to control, or was it his fingers? They were numb, as if he had touched something freezing and the coldness had penetrated him to the bone. Now it seemed that the pen was moving without any conscious effort. He gave in to the feeling and observed the result with detachment. There was an arm stretched high, reaching for the edge of— what? He found himself making a small webbed appendage on the end of the arm, where the hand should have been.

"I like the way you draw," said the nurse.

"Thanks," he said. "I haven't done this in a long time."

This one might turn out to be something. It just might.

First time in how long?

If I do it over on good paper, try a wash around everything but the head, use my felt-tips to—

"Yeah," she said, "the way you hold the pen. You're not going to get writer's cramp."

He felt the wind go out of his sails.

"That's hospital property, though. Why don't you use that nice tablet the policeman gave you?"

176

She pushed the cart out into the hall. From here the eggs now looked like two bloodshot eyes covered with cataracts.

The police drawing, he thought. Sure. That I can handle. Only . . .

Maybe if I give it one more try, relax, let it happen . . .

His fingers had a mind of their own.

He let them return to the picture on the napkin. It wasn't quite right. It shouldn't be black, not the whole thing. Parts of it, yes. But the white parts should be dripping as it struggles to get up over the white surface. It keeps slipping back into the water—into the bathtub, that is—until . . .

He saw what he was drawing, and was horrified.

I should have known, he thought, and not bothered. It's the only thing that comes out, whenever I try.

He balled up the napkin and dropped it on the floor. Then he propped up the police sketchpad again and looked at the face on the page. The eyes were staring at him.

"That's him!"

Lissa had come into the room.

"It's Christopher, isn't it?" she said. "The eyes."

"They asked me to make a sketch."

177

"Well, it looks just like him."

"It's not finished." He put the tablet aside.

"How are you?" she said gently.

She moved her hand over the bandage on the side of his head with impossibly light fingers. It reminded him of a dream he had had when he was a boy. In the dream, a girl he liked in the sixth grade, Sherron Schumacher, passed by his desk on the way to the pencil sharpener, paused, leaned down, and kissed him on the cheek. In all the years since, he had not ever been touched quite so exquisitely.

"I'm okay."

"Sure you are. You've got a broken toe, a concussion . . . Are you dizzy?"

"That's not new."

She laughed, standing close. She was wearing something crisp and white. The clean, fresh scent of her opened his nostrils.

"Where's Will?" he asked.

"Hold on, I think you're bleeding." She picked up the napkin with nervous hands, frowned at the black marks on it, folded it and daubed at his cheekbone. "Didn't they take stitches?"

"I need to talk to him. Where is he?"

"Jack, I don't know."

"What do you mean? Haven't you seen him?"

"No."

He stopped her hand. "Why not?"

She dipped a corner of the napkin in water and squeezed it out, her knuckles white. Ink dripped into the glass, turning the water cloudy.

"They haven't told you anything, have they?"

"Nobody's told me shit," he said.

"Will's . . . missing. Since last night. We don't know where he is."

"That's great. That's just fucking great."

He couldn't look at her. Outside, the street was deserted. The shopkeepers had not bothered to open up; they were home, sleeping it off, as if nothing had happened. For them, for everyone else, nothing was changed. The world would go on whether Will or the boy were alive in it or not.

"Do one thing for me," he said.

"If I can."

"Get me the hell out of here."

He heard her make a sound in her throat.

Lissa's fingers dug into his shoulders, as she buried her face in his hair to keep from crying.

179

They made a path where there was none. Coming down out of the hills, the man swung him over rocks and tree stumps, tumbleweeds, holes that opened into tunnels where animals slept by day. Then fences and retaining walls and backyards, between houses, across lots mined with sinkholes. Behind sash windows, grandparents chewed soup and sat staring into corners where nothing moved. A dog yapped from a slanted porch, then slunk away, its tail tucked between its hind legs.

Are you tired?

Yes.

Take my strength for your own.

Christopher recognized a row of houses at the edge of town, a dirty white sky and a leaden horizon, a gas station on one corner and a traffic signal swinging over crumbling pavement. He had been here with boys whose faces he couldn't remember, like the figures who walk with you in dreams.

If you let me go now, he thought, I won't tell.

Too late for that.

180

No, it isn't. I'll hide, sleep in doorways again, and never say a word . . .

It will find you.

What?

The evil.

The man opened his heavy coat and took the boy inside so their shadow was one, a trick of light and darkness. They stayed off the streets, moving parallel to the town. Once a black-and-white police car prowled silent as a shark through the reefs of strip malls and storefronts, as though pacing them from the other end of the alleys that connected with Main. When they finally entered they were like a shadow on the walls of buildings, the shadow that no one sees.

They did not slow down or stop till they came to the back of a painted building with a high, curved roof. Then the man let him out from under the coarse folds.

You must wait here, until it is finished.

Here . . . ?

There is nowhere else.

But—but I don't want you to go, the boy thought, confused.

I can't take you there.

The tall man knocked on the delivery door. Even before he turned, Christopher could not see his face, so high above the coat's collar that only wild black hair showed against the sky. From so far below, there was never anything more to see. For Christopher, for any child he would always be the tall man, the dark man, the man with no face.

Wait for me.

9.

Leanne kept her hands in her coat.

She took short, quick steps between the car and the emergency entrance. The texture changed underfoot: first blacktop, then cement, then the ribs of the rubber mat on the raised wheelchair ramp. She had never noticed such things before.

The doors did not open automatically. She had hoped they would. She made fists and felt Kleenex shredding, a gum wrapper folding into a pill-sized ball, her keys cold as nails. Luckily an intern was on his way out and held the door for her so she didn't have to touch it.

Inside the building the floor was slick, reflecting a glossy but wavering view of the hall ahead in its unevenly waxed surface, as though distorted through a layer of antique glass. There was no one at the information counter. Colored stripes ran along the wall, directing visitors to various parts of the hospital. She wondered which one was meant for her.

She chose red and followed it around the corner and past the elevators, the floor smooth and unchanging, her feet safe and protected in her shoes, her hands already unclenching in her pockets.

She saw a Sheriff's Deputy lingering outside one of the rooms, making notes on a yellow pad.

"Excuse me," she said. "I'm looking for Jack Martin."

He was young, crewcut, the sort who deliver groceries and mow lawns in the summer and refuse to accept tips.

"You are . . . . ?"

"Mrs.—Mrs. Martin." She almost stuttered over the words, as unfamiliar as stones in her mouth.

He puzzled. "Mrs. John Martin?"

"Yes, that's right. John." On his driver's license, she thought.

The young officer consulted his notes for answers, did not find them. "He's, uh, got a visitor right now."

"He does?" She tried to see around him.

"She says . . ." He faltered.

"She?"

Leanne went to the door.

One bed had a curtain drawn closed around it. She thought that must be the one, because there was a woman with shoulder-length brown hair leaning over the only other bed. She had her arms around the patient.

Sorry, Leanne almost said as she started for the other bed.

Before she could get to the curtain she saw the sketchpad and pens on the bed by the window.

The woman broke the embrace. She had on a white blouse, a sweater thrown loosely over her shoulders with the sleeves tied in front, preppie-style, a woven leather belt, and jeans.

Jack was sitting up facing the open window blinds, his back to the room. A patch of gauze was taped to one side of his head. It was only a small patch.

"It's all right," said the other woman. "I was just leaving."

She was young, though not as young as the way she dressed, late twenties at best. She was pretty enough, Leanne supposed, if you

185

liked that sort of thing. She had a vague smile that was open to practically any interpretation. It was her best feature and had no doubt taken her far. There was a scratch mark on her face that had just started to scab, poor thing. She hadn't even made the effort to cover it with makeup. Better be careful, Leanne thought, or you'll end up with a nice permanent scar there.

"So was I," Leanne said.

Jack moved his head around as slowly as an old dog caught with a spring lamb in its jaws.

"Lee?"

"Go on with what you were doing."

"Come in, Lee."

"Some other time. It will wait."

They look good together, she thought. How nice. Well, let her take care of him, his moods and depressions, all the brilliant work he's going to do someday if only the cold, cruel world would stop trying to make him grow up. Watch out, though, for the con. It's the worst kind, because he believes it himself. You think you're strong enough? You don't know what it feels like to be manipulated by a pro.

The young deputy was no longer outside

the door. He was down the hall, conferring with a heavyset man in a polyester suit.

Leanne went directly to the elevator.

The heavyset man beat her to it. He had a crewcut, too, though he was much older. His cheeks and neck were red, surely from high blood pressure rather than too much sun. Santa Claus, she thought, without the beard. You're early this year.

"Chief Pennington," he said, "Shadow Bay Police. May I have a word with you, Mrs. Martin?"

"I suppose—yes, of course."

She started to return the handshake, brought her hand half out of her coat pocket, but he was already showing her along the corridor.

"We can talk in my office. It's just down the street."

"Honey?"

"Ma'am?"

"Do you have any honey?"

"Ma'am, I'm afraid I don't."

"That's all right, then. Sugar is fine."

The Chief sat back in his swivel chair,

holding a file folder by the bottom edge as though it were a menu. He stared at it without opening the cover.

"Mrs. Martin?"

"Yes?" Hearing herself called that again, Leanne felt odd, unsure for a second whom he meant, but the feeling passed.

Still the man did not look at her.

"I would have sent someone out to talk to you, but I have two men on vacation this week, and one out sick. It's a small department."

He placed the folder on the desk and clasped his hands above his belt. She noticed that he wore an ornate black-and-gold ring on the third finger of his left hand. Then he turned the chair a few degrees to one side and gazed out the window.

"It's unusually slow this year. Or it was, until two days ago. That's why I let them have time off."

"I see."

"Not like it used to be. The movie people, up from L.A. They came here a lot. Some of them had houses. The holidays were the worst—especially with the teenagers, out to raise hell. But now, we don't get much of that. They must have found someplace else."

He wants to put me at ease, she thought. So he can trip me up. About what?

"I'd say Santa Cruz," said the Chief, idly twisting the ring on his finger.

"Oh?"

"Santa Cruz, that's my guess. Is that where they go now?"

"I suppose so."

He was not going to look at her, she decided. Why? Was he shy?

She was aware of the light flickering as a shadow passed over her; she turned her head to the window as someone walked by on the sidewalk. Across the street, the promenade of Spanish-style tourist shops appeared deserted with their dark, open doorways and still-life windows. Within the silversmith's shop, a disembodied hand rearranged turquoise buckles and Indian sand paintings.

She turned back to catch the Chief sneaking a peek at her. He lowered his eyes, brought the folder close to his face.

"Mrs. Martin, I have a couple of questions. It won't take long."

"Yes, all right." Then, when he paused to go over his papers, she said, "May I ask *you* something?"

"Please do."

"What happened to him?"

189

"You mean no one's told you?"

"I received a call this morning about an accident. That's all I know."

"That would be the Santa Mara County Sheriff. They're overseeing the investigation."

"The investigation?"

"Mr. Martin sustained minor injuries while trying to prevent a kidnapping, as I understand it. He's had a busy weekend."

"Is he going to be all right?"

"I'd say so, yes, ma'am."

"Fine. That's fine, then."

A kidnapping?

"Do—do you have any leads?"

"How do you mean?"

"On the kidnapping."

"We're working on it."

"Do you think there's a connection?"

He was waiting for her to continue, and she felt foolish. She tried to think of the right way to put it. She wanted to sound concerned, but not inordinately so.

"I mean with the child yesterday."

"A terrible thing . . ."

"And the other one."

"Do you think there is?"

"No. I mean, I have no idea. I was just

wondering. The one on Friday—the news said it was mutilated."

"The drowning? We have Parks and Recreation to thank for that one. They won't pay for a year-round lifeguard."

Drowning. She wondered why she felt so relieved.

"Toothmarks."

She stiffened. "What did you say?"

"I'll have the coroner's report later today. But I think we'll find toothmarks."

"I don't understand."

"Sharks. She'd been in the water a long time. What was left of her."

"Oh. Is that usually the case?"

"Usually?"

"Well, the others . . ."

"What others?" he said defensively.

"There was one last summer, wasn't there?"

"I'm afraid I'm not at liberty to discuss that. It's under investigation."

He returned to his folder.

"You live on Buccaneer Way, Mrs. Martin?"

"What? Yes."

She ran through the basics about her marriage, the move to Shadow Bay, the house they had bought, the separation.

"Children?"

"No," she said quickly.

"And your husband is . . ." He read from the report. "An artist? What kind of art would that be?"

"What kind?" That seemed like a strange question. "Magazine illustrations, mostly. And book covers."

"What sort of books?"

She started to say *horror* but caught herself. "Mysteries. Fantasy. Some science fiction. A little bit of everything." Would that satisfy him? "Why do you ask?"

"We have quite a few artists in the area. Might I have seen your husband's work?"

"I doubt it." That came out harder than she intended. "It's commercial work. For publication."

He wrote something down. "Would that include men's magazines?"

"What do you mean?"

"*Playboy*, that sort of thing?"

"Some, I guess. In the beginning."

He was hiding his face almost completely behind the folder now. "*Penthouse?*"

"I think so."

"Any others?"

She searched her memory. "Let me see.

Cavalier, Rogue, Escapade . . . Most of that was before we were married."

"*Hustler?*"

"No, not *Hustler.*"

"Did he specialize?"

"In what way?"

"A particular kind of model, say."

"He wasn't a photographer."

"But he worked from photographs?"

"Sometimes."

"Did he prefer brunettes? Blondes? Tall, short? Old? Young?"

She didn't like the way this was going. "I told you, he did illustrations for stories. They were assignments. Not the kind of pictures you mean."

"Do you have any of those magazines? I'd be interested in seeing them, if you do."

I'll bet you would, she thought. "No, I don't. You'll have to ask Jack about that. I hadn't seen or spoken to him for almost a year, until the other night. I'm sorry, but I don't know what you're getting at. I thought you wanted a statement. About what happened."

"I do."

"Well, it sounds like you're more interested in my husband." My soon-to-be ex-husband, she thought. "If you are, I can't help you."

He closed the folder and squared it up on his desk. Then he sat back and looked out at the promenade, the antique store and gift shop and tourist bureau, all the shadowed doorways and wavery windows with no one moving behind them.

"I hope you don't take this in the wrong way," he said. "I'm only doing my job."

Still he hadn't asked her anything about herself, about her part in the other night. But she had the feeling he had asked what he really wanted to know.

She picked up her purse. "I think I'd like to go."

He did not deny her request. At last he dared to look at her full on. His eyes took in every detail, as if measuring her against some secret dossier. She remained in her chair, held there by his unnatural attention.

"One more question."

"Yes?"

"Have you ever been to Kansas City?" he asked, twisting his ring.

What? Had she heard him correctly? "Not that I . . . no. I don't believe so."

She had to get away from the pressure of his gaze. It was too much; she felt herself being handled, marked to fit the needs of his private agenda. Outside, there was a clattering. She turned to the window for relief. A bag lady wove across the bricked street, pushing a shopping cart full of cans and newspapers. As she reached the near curb the clattering stopped, and a boy dodged around her on the sidewalk, walking fast, coming this way.

"I was there once," he said. "It was shortly after my wife passed away . . . I took the Super Chief to a law enforcement convention in Chicago. We had a two-hour layover in Kansas City, at the old Union Station. There was a young lady on a bench, waiting, I presume, for her train. She was sitting there sipping a Coca-Cola and reading *Cosmopolitan Magazine*. She couldn't have been more than eighteen or nineteen— the flush of youth was still on her cheeks. I saw her for only a moment, on my way to the gate, but I have never forgotten that face. It was the most beautiful I have ever seen. She didn't see me, which was just as well, because I wouldn't have had the courage to speak to her. I knew it then, and I know it to this day . . .

"For a moment, when you first walked out of the hospital room, Mrs. Martin, I wondered if you could be that same young lady. But it isn't possible, is it? You're not old enough. Please forgive me. I'm a foolish man. I'm sorry to have taken up so much of your time."

She was speechless.

She tilted her head at the Chief across the spare, compulsively neat desktop. Somewhere a dull, muffled ringing began. It was not the shopping cart against the bricks but the loose earthen tiles in the eaves above the arcade across the street, lifting and falling like the plates of a xylophone as a late-morning sea breeze swept inland. Suddenly she saw the boy standing there on the other side of the glass, trying to see in. Their eyes met. He drew back, startled.

She was breathing so fast that the wheezing started up in her chest again. She put a hand to her mouth, afraid that she might begin to cough uncontrollably.

"Let me give you my card," the Chief said, "in case you need to get in touch with me."

"Thank you."

Without realizing what she was doing, she removed her hand from her coat pocket. Then it was too late to avoid taking his card.

As she did so, her hand began to tingle. The edge of the card seemed as sharp and cold as a blade of ice, cutting into her finger. Then, as if crystals were freezing in her blood, pumping along her arm to her heart and brain, she felt a numbing in the middle of her chest. At the same time she saw pictures taking form, bright and clear and transparent, superimposed on the air in front of her. The images came in fragments, incomplete, each one shattering and falling as the next one took its place.

She was in a darkening forest. She looked down and saw the legs and lower body of a man running through tangled underbrush. There was something wrong with one of the legs. He dragged it and swung it forward again laboriously with each step, as if carrying a great weight, slogging through vines and over fallen trees. The toe of the shoe stuttered and caught on something in the mud. Then a thick tuber grew up from the earth and wrapped around the ankle. He lost his footing as more tendrils brought him to his knees. Then she saw that they were short white arms with human hands and blackened fingernails that hooked into his skin as they snaked up over his body. The man could not throw them off.

On one of his hands, the left, was a large black-and-gold ring.

"No," she said, dropping the Chief's business card into her purse and wrenching free of the dark, shining images.

"Ma'am?"

"Nothing," she said. "It's nothing."

The Chief looked at her curiously. "Are you sure?"

"You haven't been in the hills yet, have you?"

"The hills? No, ma'am, not for a long time. Is there some reason I should?"

"I was—thinking about the hills. They can be treacherous, if you don't know the way."

"Is that how you injured your hand?"

She noticed the adhesive bandage across her palm.

"No. I—I cut myself. At home."

"An accident?"

"Yes. An accident."

"Not serious, I hope."

"No, not serious. But you can't be too careful. You have to watch what you touch, and where you step."

"I'll do that."

She closed her purse and stood.

"I hope your husband is more careful, too, from now on. When he leaves the hospital, will he be going back to Eden Cove?"

"I would imagine." How did the Chief

know that Jack had been staying in the Cove? "Did I tell you that?"

The Chief didn't answer.

Without thinking she said, "He's not in any kind of trouble, is he?"

The Chief took a long time. "No, ma'am."

That's good, she thought. I won't have to worry about a lawyer for him. Not Steve, of course, but someone else where she worked. Did the Chief know about that, too?

There was an awkward moment as he opened the door for her.

"Thank you again, Mrs. Martin."

He held his eyes down. When she left he nodded politely, almost bowing.

The small waiting room was empty except for another young crewcut police officer, poking away at a computer terminal, a sketch before him. He did not look up. At the door, the nervous boy she had seen outside the window waited for her to leave. He had clear gray eyes and an intelligent face. Like Jack, she thought. Or the way he must have been, when he was that age.

Part Four
The Rain

10.

On weekends the Alcazar Theater opened at noon. Today, Sunday, there was almost no one in line. An elderly couple with money and seniors' passes in hand waited for admission to *Angel's Flight*, a man wearing a raincoat and a razor-cut toupée paced by the poster for a sexy thriller, *Under the Skin*, while no one at all was here to see the science fiction comedy *Is Anybody There?* The last line led to a double feature, *American Zombie* and *The Hungry Dead*, and it was here that Robby, Kevin and Jamie were to meet David for the first showing of the day.

Sitting with their backbones to the wall by the ticket booth, waiting for the multiplex to open, they appeared gloomy and doom-ridden, like young recruits on a last fling before a mission into enemy territory. Their pallor was even more pronounced than usual, their fingernails colorless, their clothing drab and washed-out in the chill morning air.

Jamie had a bully's build under his flannel shirt, with stubby fingers and short, dirty hair. Kevin, with his choirboy's face and gawky neck, wore the constant half-smile of secret knowledge, as if he had just won a replay on a pinball machine and was waiting for the world to notice. And Robby, all of five feet tall, had the defiant, pugnacious attitude of a boy who is always the last one chosen for any team and wants to be sure people know that he doesn't care. In David's absence they might as soon take up snatching purses or torturing cats. At the moment David was not here, the movie theater was not yet open, and they were running out of patience.

For now, Jamie turned without enthusiasm to the latest issue of *Shock Zone Magazine*.

"I saw that," said Kevin, pointing to a production still from *The Return of the Boogeyman*.

"It sucked," said Robby.

Jamie thumbed to another page.

"Remember *Don't Turn On the Lights?*" said Kevin.

"Yeah," said Robby, "it ate the big one."

On the next page was a layout from Stuart Gordon's remake of *Caltiki, the Immortal Monster.*

"I want to see that," said Kevin.

"It sucks donkey dicks," said Robby.

"How do *you* know?"

"You guys," said Jamie, "I'm reading, all right?"

Just then a young woman in an ugly, ill-fitting uniform lowered the plywood inside the ticket booth. She finished counting down the cash drawer, tested the ticket machine and faced forward, glassy-eyed.

The boys were first up.

In the lobby, the air had the sour tinge of a catbox that needs to be changed. The old carpet was badly worn, the pile teased into temporary arousal by a vacuum cleaner that had left lawnmower rows on the nappy surface. Recycled popcorn warmed under a lightbulb, candy bars faded behind glass, ice cream grew whiskers in a case crusted with white ice, a cloudy umbrella of Orange Bang sprayed the inside of a clear plastic dispenser, while uncooked hot dogs pale as sev-

205

ered fingers rolled under a heat lamp, sweating fat.

There were four doors leading to four auditoriums. The elderly couple helped each other to the first one, while the raincoat man bought a tub of oily popcorn and headed for the second. Door number three was locked. The boys went into number four and took seats close to the screen, leaving one row in front of them so they could prop up their feet.

No one else came in.

"Where is everybody?" said Kevin.

"They're scared," Robby told him. "All those little kids, afraid of the . . ." He stopped himself.

"The what?"

"Nothin'."

"He isn't *real*, you know," said Kevin.

"Duh," said Robby.

"Then why don't you say it?"

"The Man With No Face, okay?"

"Okay."

"It's just stuff they tell kids so they'll stay home."

"My mom and dad never told me that."

"Mine, neither."

"Nobody has to tell them anything, this time," said Jamie.

206

They fell silent.

They were alone in the cold auditorium. For weeks the audience for films like *Deadspace* and *Something Dark* and *The Light Under the Door* and *Ernest Goes to Hell* had steadily diminished. Except for a few teenagers, the boys had the screening room to themselves lately. The younger ones who always ran up and down the aisles and threw candy and sneaked into all the other movies without paying now stayed home, whether by choice or parental decree. Last week the boys had said very little, and the pictures had seemed different somehow. It was as if something more than the other kids had gone away.

"What would happen," Kevin said, "if we didn't come? Would they show the movies anyway?"

"They'd be pretty stupid if they did," said Robby.

"But if nobody was here . . ."

"Then who cares?"

"No, I mean, if they showed the picture, and nobody was here, would there *be* a picture?"

"Why don't you sneak in and find out?"

"Well, if I saw it, it would be."

"You sure are dumb," said Robby. "If you see it, it's there. If you don't, it's not. Get it?"

"But what if *no* one sees it? What do you think, Jamie?"

"Ask David. What time is it?"

Robby held his big wristwatch close to his face. The only light came from a hidden fixture in the back wall and the green EXIT sign at the side.

"Five more minutes. I'm gonna get some Skittles."

"Get me some, too," said Kevin. "Or Bon Bons. No, a Klondike Bar."

"Got any money?"

"I'll pay you back."

"Sure, you will."

"I promise."

"And a Pepsi," said Jamie.

"What size?"

"Monster Gulp."

"They don't have Pepsi. Only Coke and orange."

"Okay, Coke."

"And a Twix," said Kevin.

"And a Tobler."

"And Red Hots."

"And Raisinets, and Junior Mints, and Hot Tamales, and—"

"Sure," said Robby. "In your dreams."

Behind them, the door to the lobby opened and a puff of cold air ran down the aisle and under the seats. Then the door whispered shut.

"You better jam," said Jamie.

"I'm *going*, okay?"

The rest of the theater still appeared to be empty.

"Want me to go with you?" said Kevin.

"No way."

Robby's shoes unpeeled like suction cups from the sticky floor, then stuck to the synthetic fibers of the carpeting in the aisle. At the back wall, a shadow grew arms and legs, an octopus concealed in a protective cloud of darkness. It was a teenage couple. They had come into the theater a moment ago and were already going at it, unable to wait for the show to start.

In the lobby, a few new arrivals milled about the candy counter. A high school girl in a dingy uniform moved sleepily behind the case, pumping a dispenser with the heel of her hand, squirting mustard-colored cheese sauce thick as pus over a paper plate of tortilla chips.

"Gimme a . . ."

She handed the plate to a biker with a bandana tied around his head, then tried to focus her eyes on Robby.

"Gimme a—a Sugar Babies," he said. "And a Tobler and, uh, some Red Hots. And a Klondike Bar. And a Pepsi. I mean Coke."

She did not seem to be able to find his face, though there was no one else at this end of the counter. She opened the case and set out the items on the glass, moving in dreamlike slow motion.

"Anything else?" Her voice came from the general vicinity of her mouth.

"That's all," said Robby. "How much?"

Perplexed, she sought an answer from the price list by the cash register. "Um, just a minute," she said.

"A hot dog, please," said an unshaven man with gray skin.

"Chili?"

"Relish."

"One relish dog. Onions?"

"Please."

She extracted a bun from a plastic bag, found the tongs and held them under the heat lamp, dowsing for a wrinkled wiener.

Robby picked up his candy.

"And my drink," he said.

She had forgotten he was there. "Medium, large or . . . ?"

"Monster Gulp."

"And an orange drink," said the man with gray skin.

"One Monster orange."

"Medium," said the man.

"Make mine medium, too," said Robby, counting his money.

"A medium orange?"

"Coke," said Robby.

The man swaddled his hot dog in napkins. "Where's the relish?"

"Yes, sir." She uncovered a tray of relish that looked like seaweed in aspic. Then she rang up the gray man's order and made change.

"Hey," said Robby, "the movie's gonna start."

"Popcorn and a Diet Seven-Up," someone else said.

"What size?"

Robby didn't wait. He plunked a wadded-up bill on the case, all he had, pocketed the candy and stole away before she noticed. He glanced over his shoulder as he crossed the lobby, and bumped into the wall.

There was the door in front of him. He did a disappearing act, easing it open a few inches and scooting inside.

He was late. The house lights were off and

the movie was already in progress. The picture on the screen was a night scene, not bright enough to show him the way back to his seat. His hand made contact with a fuzzy armrest. He slipped sideways in front of it and sat down long enough for his eyes to adjust.

Gradually the other seatbacks became visible, lines of velour upholstery that took on a sheen like cat fur in moonlight. One row, two, three, four . . . all the way down to the screen.

All empty.

Kevin and Jamie had gone out after him. To the snack bar. Or the men's room.

Or they had moved.

Where?

A meadow of glowing seats lay before him. After a minute he was sure that there were no heads showing.

He was alone in the theater.

Then, in the semi-darkness, someone coughed.

Robby turned his head.

There in the corner, against the back wall, a shadow moved.

"Okay, guys, I see you," said Robby.

The shadow shifted position, grew larger.

"Jamie? Kev?"

It wasn't his friends. The shadow had been there in the corner, before. The two teen-agers making out. That was what it was.

"'Scuse me," said Robby. "I thought—"

The shadow in the corner expanded, flow-ing up over the seats, moving sinuously along the back wall and across the aisle, coming toward him.

"You thought what?" whispered a voice, almost a hiss, as the shadow settled into the seat next to his.

Robby glued his eyes to the screen.

The camera was panning slowly across soft, pinkish-blue hills. Somewhere out of the frame, a woman moaned. The landscape be-came a body, a woman's body. A hand the size of an Amazonian tarantula walked up her bare thigh to her waist, then stroked the underside of a mammoth breast.

"What do you think now? Do you like what you see?"

This wasn't *American Zombie*. The camera panned higher. There was Uma Thurman's face, the sleek forehead and engorged, tu-mescent lips, exactly as she appeared on the poster for *Under the Skin*.

"I don't think nothin'. I'm in the wrong place."

A hairy hand measured Robby's knee.

213

"Are you sure?"

"Yeah. 'Bye."

The hand clamped his kneecap.

"Hey, get yer paws . . ."

Robby's shoulders were enfolded by an arm inside heavy black cloth, as the raincoat opened.

Robby pushed away, scissored his legs over the other armrest, fell into the seat on his right and crawled over the floor to the aisle. He was on his feet by the time he got out the door to the lobby.

He scuttled quickly to the next door, reached for the handle.

"Where do you think you're going?"

A strong hand bracketed the top of his head so that he could not run.

"Come with me, young man!"

He was dragged along the lobby wall. A stout man with hardly any hair and bulging eyes held him against the framed COMING AT-TRACTIONS poster for *Up From the Depths*. It was Mr. Fons, the manager.

"I didn't do nothin', Mr. Fons. I went in the wrong door, is all."

"You should be careful about doors. Some of them are definitely *off-limits*!"

Fons was completely pushed out of shape, breathing so hard it looked like fire was about to shoot out of his nose, his face greased with sweat as heavy as Vaseline.

"I'm *sorry*, okay?"

The manager released him and adjusted his Coke-bottle eyeglasses. He tested door number three to be sure it was locked securely.

Robby had tried to get in the wrong door this time, too.

"Aren't you gonna open it?"

"Theater number three is . . . out of order."

"What if somebody wants to—?"

"I said, it's out of order! Do you understand English?"

Fons shouted so loudly the people at the candy counter stopped what they were doing, frozen like shooting gallery targets.

In the sudden silence, Robby said sweetly, "What are you so mad about, Mr. Fons?"

Everybody was looking. To cover himself, the manager said, "You tried to sneak into theater number two without paying."

"I told you, I made a mistake."

"Not only that, it's an NC–17 booking. That's against the law."

"What are you gonna do, arrest me? *American Zombie*'s R-rated. So's *The Hungry Dead*. You let me in—I got a ticket to prove it.

Just like *Horror House of Blood,* and *They,* and all those other pictures!"

The manager smoothed the top of his head and made a gesture for Robby to lower his voice. "Those films aren't primarily sexual in content," he said, his vocal cords tight.

"No, but they're against the law for kids, too. . . . I know why you let us in. Because if we didn't come, nobody'd be here except the perverts and creepazoids like that guy in number two, and then there wouldn't *be* any more pictures, and you'd be out on your butt!"

The girl from the candy counter came over, wiping her nose, looking like death warmed over.

"Mr. Fons, we're out of Coke. Can you get me some more?"

"Not now, Shelley! Can't you see I'm busy?"

"Yes, sir . . ."

Fons moved in close, blocking Robby from her view. There were imitation-butter stains on his shirt and his tie needed to be ironed.

"What pervert?" he said. "What are you talking about?"

"Take a look," said Robby. "He's in there right now. Got a black raincoat on. Only it's missin' a coupla buttons, know what I mean?"

Robby flipped up the collar of his shirt. A box of Red Hots fell out of his breast pocket.

"I paid for it," he said nonchalantly. "If anybody says I didn't, they're lyin'."

"Shelley, do you have your flashlight?"

"Yes, Mr. Fons . . ."

"I want you to look in theater number two." He kept his back to the door and held it open for her. "Tell me what you see."

"A tit, sir . . . I mean, a breast."

"What else?"

"Nothing, Mr. Fons . . ."

He took the flashlight and swept the interior for himself. The light reflected off the screen, bleaching out a stippled section of Uma Thurman's vastly protruberant nipple. All the seats were empty now, even the back row.

"He was there," said Robby.

"Was he?" Fons said weakly, for the first time addressing Robby without the slightest touch of sarcasm or anger, as if unsure which prospect was the more disturbing, that the man had been there earlier or that now he was nowhere to be seen.

"I swear to God," said Robby.

"Mr. Fons," said Shelley, "your necktie just fell off."

"Thank you. Now run along," he said, not looking at either Robby or the girl. It was not clear whether he meant one or the other or both of them.

"Hey . . . are you sure you paid for that?" Shelley tapped the box of Red Hots in Robby's hand.

"Run along, I said!"

"Yes, sir . . ." said Shelley.

"What are *you* looking at?" said Fons.

Robby smiled as he nudged the necktie with the toe of his Reebok. It lay there like a snakeskin on the virgules of the carpet, the knot at its head practically cut through, hanging by a thread.

"Nothing," Robby said, and took his time walking casually back to door number four.

Jamie and Kevin were watching *American Zombie*, the scene where the head falls off, when Robby sat down next to them.

"Here." Robby took out the Tobler and Red Hots and passed them down, then settled in. "What did I miss?"

"This guy with the haircut, he's got a Mercedes and everything, but what his girlfriend doesn't know is, he's dead."

"Guys."

It was David, in the row behind them.

"Hi, Davey," Jamie said. "Where . . . ?"

They turned around to see David's face, but there was only the outline of his head with the projection beam above it, reflected in their eyes, a pinpoint frame of moving color repeated six times, and the sound of screaming from the movie screen, now at their backs.

"I went to the police station," said David. "I told them about the body. And Chris."

"So? Did they find him, or what?"

David unfolded a sheet of paper and showed it to them. The Xerox was hard to see, but it was Christopher. The eyes stood out.

"They're looking for him. They say. Just like they looked for all the others."

"So what do we do now?"

"We find him, before somebody else does."

11.

As Leanne approached the intersection, the traffic signal started swinging like a railroad brakeman's lantern.

She was grateful for the wind. Without it she might not have noticed the red light at all. The way the mist had settled, she could hardly see the white line down the middle of the street. She tapped the brake pedal and came to a stop at the crosswalk, as a homeless woman pushed a shopping cart off the curb.

That would be just what I need, she thought. To hit a pedestrian a block from the police station, after running a red light. The Chief wouldn't let me talk my way out of this one.

The Chief . . . What an odd man. And so

interested in Jack. Why? There was something more, but he wouldn't come right out and say it.

Through the mist, she saw the signal melt from red to green, and lifted her foot from the brake.

The old woman was still in the intersection. She had stopped halfway across, her hands frozen on the shopping cart. She was looking through the windshield at Leanne.

What should I do? Honk? Drive around her? Or wait for the light to change again?

The woman left the cart and came over to the car.

Did she want a handout?

Leanne made sure the door was locked.

The old woman took out a piece of paper and pressed it to the glass. It was a Xerox of a hand-drawn face, with computer-generated lettering across the top:

HAVE YOU SEEN THIS CHILD?

Leanne recognized the sketch. Not the face but the style. It was not one of those composite Identikit drawings she had seen on WANTED posters all her life, but a real artist's rendering, with properly proportioned features, a sense of life . . .

222

It was Jack's, she was sure.

"Wait."

She lowered her window, wrinkling the paper, causing it to fold in half. There was the telephone number of the Shadow Bay Police Department at the bottom, but no signature. Jack had been drawing something in the hospital this morning, before she went to her interview with the Chief and then to lunch; she remembered his open sketchbook on the bed, the outline of what might have been a head . . . This was it.

The Chief had said something about an attempted kidnapping. Jack had been a witness. Apparently they had asked him to reproduce a likeness.

That meant he wasn't a suspect himself, didn't it?

Then what was the Chief's interest in Jack?

The wind caught the Xerox, peeling it off the glass. Before she could get her window down fully the paper blew away, yanked into the mist.

"Where did you get that?"

The woman glanced back down the street, in the direction of the police station. Her eyes were inconsolable, like those of someone who has awakened from a nightmare only to find that her house has burned down.

She can't speak, Leanne realized.

It was a good thing there were no other cars at the intersection. The woman went back to her shopping cart, which was loaded down with plastic bags, bottles, cans and bundles of newspapers, and returned with another copy of the drawing. She forced it on Leanne, thrusting it through the open window.

"Thank you." Leanne let the damp page settle on the dashboard. "I'll keep my eyes open. I'm sure they'll find him."

The old woman nodded solemnly.

She wants to help, to do her part, Leanne thought. I hope everyone in this town feels the same way.

The traffic light had gone through two cycles. Leanne waved through the glass and drove slowly forward, hoping that no other cars were concealed behind the wall of mist.

The wall dissipated as soon as she crossed the intersection, blowing on between the buildings. She passed empty sidewalks and locked storefronts. Except for a mini-mart and a movie theater around the corner off Main, Shadow Bay looked like a ghost town, a set without actors or crew. The old woman was now a receding spot in her rearview mirror, a wraith blown over the curb and up

224

an alley, leaving the street as bare as a dreamed landscape.

She came to a blinking three-way signal, and realized that she was driving in the wrong direction.

How had she managed that?

Instead of turning west out of the hospital parking lot, she had gone away from the coast, as though fleeing the mist. Actually that was not such a bad idea. The white sky behind her was darkening now as something more than mist gathered force and pressed inland.

On an impulse she chose the fork leading toward the foothills. She seemed to remember a connecting road somewhere to the south that led back down to the coast. It was the long way around, but at least she would not have to go back through the city.

The sky grew darker as trees drooped above her, closing off the sky. She was tempted to turn on her headlights. The Xeroxed drawing of the boy's face reflected in the slanted windshield, superimposed over the streets ahead. She could not escape his features, the wideset eyes and Cupid's lips, and after a few miles he became as familiar to her as a dashboard saint floating in double exposure above the rooftops.

Who are you? she thought.

Well, I hope they find you, whoever you are.

What did Jack have to do with any of this? Had he found a new career? *Jack Martin, Police Artist.* It sounded like a bad TV series.

Whatever it's about, she told herself, it's not my concern now. He's got someone else to look after him. There was no point in trying to warn him about anything. There never had been. Whatever she had seen at home this morning had obviously happened already. A bump on the head, a broken toe . . . he'd live. Even if she had seen it in time, would he have listened and believed her? Probably not. He doesn't need me; he never did. It was my conceit, nothing more, that made me think I was even an important part of his life. He locked me out a long time ago, and he'll never let me back in.

Her mind had wandered. She now found herself well past the residential streets, on her way up a side road into the foothills. Ahead was an official yellow-and-black state sign:

Lost River Landfill
CLOSED

226

It was a single-lane road with no room to turn around. She bounced on dirt, passing deadwood trees with shallow roots, blackened twigs like charred fingers reaching for her door handles. The road had not been used in some time.

After a mile or so she came to a space that would have been wide enough for a J-turn if not for the chunks of loose granite and sandstone that had tumbled down onto the shoulder from above.

She had no choice but to keep going.

Eventually the road ended at a wide bulldozed plateau. In front of her was a boarded-up tollhouse. Beyond the gate, a broad truck route led down from the other side of the plateau, presumably to the landfill.

She was about to turn around, when she noticed another road, partially obscured by a fallen branch.

Was it a fire road? If so, it probably cut along the southwest side of the hill to reconnect at some point with the coast. She was sure she had passed the other end of the road many times on the highway, going to or from work.

Was it still in use?

She got out of the car.

She moved the dead, flaking branch with

her good hand and looked down the road. It was no narrower than the one she had just driven. As far as she could see around the hillside, a considerable distance from this elevation, it was clear. That meant she would have plenty of warning if another vehicle decided to come up in the opposite direction. And of course it would take her safely away from the oppressive black sky that now hovered directly over the city.

She got back in her car and started down.

The access road carried her around the hillside in constantly diminishing fractals. Walnut, elm and birchwood trees hugged the edge, while old oaks clung like stooped sentinels on the high cliffs overhead. Then the road made a hairpin turn and she was riding the brakes in order not to go over into the densely overgrown ravine.

Someone else had not been so lucky.

At first it was a tarnished coin in tall grass, revealing itself to be something more only when she slowed to the point where she was almost not moving. Any earlier or later in the day and the ravine would have been lost in shadow, but now, briefly and only from this angle, a part of the gully was illuminated by the aluminized mirror of the sky. There was a glint of glass, then the entire back windshield of a car that had gone off the road into the bushes below. The windshield was clean and unbroken. As she set the brake, she saw tire tracks where the driver had lost control. When had it happened? Not long ago. The tread marks were still freshly minted, parallel rows of hieroglyphics scribbled hastily in the dirt.

She stood dangerously close to the edge, put her hands to her mouth and shouted.

"Hello . . . Can you hear me? Are you all right?"

Of course they were not, whoever they were. The car had gone over a cliff. She made out what she thought was the shape of a head in the front seat.

"I'll get help!"

How long might that take? A person could bleed to death before she could get down to the city and back.

"Wait . . ."

What else could they do? Stupid! If they were alive, that is. There was no answer, only the echo of her own voice across the basin.

She stepped carefully off the road and into the underbrush, then started down into the ravine. Half the time she was sliding, the other half she was holding on for dear life to the stunted, prickly bushes. Only the car it-self, when she reached it, prevented her from tumbling all the way to the bottom.

It was a maroon Mustang.

It looked familiar.

As soon as she glanced inside, she knew why.

She found a footpath and stayed on it. There was nothing else to do, no other way out of the ravine. She certainly couldn't climb back up.

After it seemed as though she had gone halfway around the mountain, she began to wonder how long she had been walking. Was it really so late? No, it was the sky. The black clouds over the city had spread here, as well, darkening the day.

Presently she heard running water, and the voices of children.

Children?

She came off the path into a clearing that was surrounded by empty cardboard boxes and shipping crates, arranged like vertical coffins in a megalithic circle.

What was this place?

230

"Welcome," someone said.

As he came into the circle and she saw his clear eyes and easy smile, the wariness left her. He was somewhere between twenty and forty. No way to tell from his clothes; they were pieced together from found items spanning several years and styles. At first she thought his hair was short and slicked back. Then she noticed the ponytail.

She said, "Please . . . Can you help me?"

"I'll try. Did you break down?"

He couldn't have mistaken her for a hiker, not with open-toed shoes and the long coat. "No," she told him, "I left my car back there." She gestured vaguely up and over her shoulder.

He smiled more broadly. Had she said the secret word?

"Does that mean you want to join us?"

His face was disarming, so open and so pleased, as if she were special in some way only he could see.

She ignored his peculiar question and went on.

"There's another car, a Mustang back about, I don't know, a mile. It went off the road. There's a man inside."

"Is he hurt?"

"I think he's dead."

231

Of course he was. His eyes were open and so was his throat and his shirt was caked with brown blood. How should she put it? She had not had to describe such a thing to anyone before.

"I'll tell the Professor."

Mystified, she followed him out of the clearing and along another path through the trees, then was astonished to find herself looking down into a huge crater. It might have been the top of a volcano.

"Is that the landfill?"

"It used to be."

On the plain below, children chased a flock of tame seagulls and mothers hung out laundry next to shacks made from tin sheeting and odds and ends of lumber. The stench was dreadful, though a relief compared to what she had discovered in the Mustang. There was a teardrop trailer, an old school bus, a couple of junked vans and a tanker truck, all modified into living quarters, as if a mobile home park had recycled itself out of the junk and rubble of an extinct civilization.

The Professor was a frail man who lived in the largest of the sheds, surrounded by more books than one person could read in a lifetime, no doubt scavenged from the landfill. The man with the ponytail left her there and

232

crossed the plain to talk to some children who were digging a hole with pointed sticks.

The Professor trembled as he sat down on the porch. She thought, He has arthritis. It must be rough on him here, with all the dampness in the air. I wonder why he stays?

She repeated the story about finding the car, the body, without going into who Will was or that she knew him. She realized that she did not know whether or not Will had a family.

"It was not an accident," said the Professor.

"How do you know that?"

"Because *he* came again last night, with his black soul and terrible sword. So many years . . . and now it begins again."

She had never liked Will that much, had found him more than a little phony, the sort of man who always tried too hard to get women on his side, as if he didn't really trust them. Jack had liked him, though. One of the many inscrutabilities of their marriage. But *black soul? Terrible sword?*

He called across to the thin man with the ponytail.

"Get two strong men and take care of it. Quickly—before the rain!"

Take care of it. Did that mean report it to

233

the authorities, or hide it before anyone else saw it?

The thin man came back with his arms around two children.

"Sam and Deirdre want to bury him," he said to the Professor. "They'd like to hold a memorial service, and say a few words."

"Is that right?"

"He was my favorite," said Deirdre.

"Mine, too," said the boy.

"Then it's proper that you should honor him. When you have finished, you may speak your heart. But hurry—the night is coming."

"Thank you!" they said, and ran off.

This was crazy. They were going to bury Will? Two children, with sticks? They knew him?

Then Leanne saw the broken body of a seagull laid out on a plastic sheet near where they were digging. It did not seem to have a head.

"What happened?"

"We had a visitor," said the younger man.

"Tell the others to break camp," said the Professor. "We must leave by nightfall."

The younger man nodded and cast his eyes down. He was not disagreeing, but he obviously felt ambivalent about the prospect.

"Some of them won't want to go, Barton . . ."

"Tell them *he* has come back."

Who, she wondered, were they talking about?

"And he will come again, with his sacks and his shovels. We are no longer safe here."

Two steps forward, stop, stand on one foot, touch your toe behind your back, two more steps, stop, pat your crotch, take another step . . .

"Ask Reno," said David.

"Go on, Robby."

"Yeah . . . !"

The street in front of the theater was darker than it should have been for this early in the afternoon, with what precious little light that still showed in the sky choked off by the eaves of the Spanish tile roofs. At the end of the sidestreet, the sky above Main was black as a rotting mushroom, with purple gills on the western horizon, where the rain had already started.

Reno, the Dreadlock Man, crossed the intersection and continued blissfully on his daily journey to the waterfront, unconcerned that he was walking into rather than away from the wrathful heart of the storm.

Take another step, stop, stand on one foot, kick your heel up and reach behind your back, two more steps, stop, pat your crotch, take two steps . . .

"Hey, Reno, wait up!"

Robby got to the corner several strides ahead of the others.

"My little men," said Reno, showing sand-bag teeth. "What you been up to, watchin' the dirty picture show?"

"It wasn't dirty," said Jamie. "It was horror."

"Well, that can be dirty, too, you know. All that killing and such, it ain't a pretty sight. I had a cousin, he lost an arm in the sugar combine. 'Twasn't any fun, believe me . . ."

"Reno," said David, "do you remember the other one, the one who walks with us?"

"The baby! I see his picture all over town today."

"Do you know where he is?"

"Well now, I thought I seen him with a man this mornin'."

"Where?"

"Right here on Beechwood. They was walkin', and then they wasn't here no more."

"Where did they go?"

"That's the mystery question now, ain't it?"

"We have to find him, Reno."

"You and the whole po-lice force." Reno leaned down and spoke confidentially, the grasshopper bending over the ants. "He in trouble, ain't he?"

"Well . . ." Jamie began.

"Yes," said David. "We have to get to him before anyone else does."

"Seems like somebody already did."

"Who's the man?" said David, "and where is he now?"

"You can always ask Eleanor. She don't talk much, remember . . . but her eyes, my boy, her *eyes*!"

12.

Eleanor Rigby was what people called her, though no one could say for sure where she came from or if any part of that was really her name. Something had happened to her somewhere down the line, something too fierce for her to talk about, and she had landed here, discarded, tossed into a far corner like a set of keys to a house that no longer exists.

She lived by her wits and with the help of others like her—Buffalo Bob, who got off a bus one day, cashed in his ticket, drank it all the first afternoon and had been here ever since; Weejun, who wore only one shoe because he had six toes on one foot and wanted everyone to see his only source of pride; and Danny Apple, an ex-jockey from down south

239

who got himself in wrong with a racetrack fix and took it on the lam—except that no one was like Eleanor. As far as anyone knew she had never spoken. She might have been sixty, she might have been fifty, she might have been thirty-five; a year on the streets can be like ten under a roof. She carried all she had in her shopping cart, sorted cans and bottles by day for the recycling machine, found a stairwell or a doorway at night, never sleeping in one place for too many times running. It was the police she feared, or hated, or both. They had betrayed her in her other life, and so she kept one step ahead of them on her nightly rounds.

Robby saw her first, at the end of an alley off Greenworth, where Reno had said she would be. She was on a loading bay, trying to get her cart up after her so it would be protected when the rains came.

He ran back half a block and told the others.

The air was cooler by twenty degrees now, the sun little more than a memory, the streets bleak and deserted. Cars passed rarely, those that did with windows up and headlights on, speeding to make every traffic signal between here and home. Kevin and Jamie went into the alley ahead of David, who paused to check the skyline one more time. The rooftops at the end of Main were blackening under a sky that cracked with arcs of chain lightning far out at sea, the horizon already blurring where the storm had released the first wave of its attack on the long march to shore. David raised his collar and went into the alley after his friends.

"Hi there, uh, Eleanor!" called Robby. "Remember me? I'm Robby, and that's Kevin, and Jamie, and . . ."

Her eyes; it was true, what Reno had said. Her eyes, which had been dull, filmed over, beyond the point of caring what was on her plate, came to life as the four boys encroached on her turf. Her back straightened. It was not weak. Her hands, and they were not small, drew her coat closed and made fists. Her arms folded, her feet found their balance and her legs planted her on the landing so that she towered above them. But her eyes told the story, and it was *Don't come any closer* and *This better be good* and *You don't want to mess with me, do you? you really don't want to get into it, because if you do you won't come out of it the same as you went in,* because what was there in her eyes was something too serious, too heavy and too sad for anyone to want to know, at least anyone who had a choice.

Robby said, "I seen you lots of times, down by the dock . . . Here, want some Sugar Babies?"

"Where is he?" said David.

She didn't move another muscle, stopped breathing, didn't blink. Watching him.

"You know who I mean, don't you?"

Very slowly she unfolded her arms. Reached into the cart. Under the plastic bags. Feeling for something.

Her arm jutted out, elbow locked. In her hand was a HAVE YOU SEEN THIS CHILD? poster. The one with Christopher's face.

"Yeah," said Robby, "that's him."

"We want to know what happened to him," said David. "If he's all right. Reno said you could help us."

Behind her, on the loading bay, at the corner of the locked-down steel door, a shadow moved. It stood up, taller than she was, and came forward. To the edge of the concrete.

"She don't talk," said Buffalo Bob, the bouquet of the grape wafting down to them.

Another shadow on the wall metamorphosed into a man with ropy arms, spindly legs and only one shoe.

"Not that way," he said.

A dirtpile halfway down the alley twisted to life like a golliwog with fat, round body and short, bony limbs.

"Sometimes we talk for her," Danny Apple said. "If she wants us to."

"Does she know where Christopher is?"

She shook her head from side to side, not waiting for them to answer for her.

"Does someone have him?"

She didn't move.

"She doesn't know."

"Then," said David, "where is the man?"

"What man?" said Weejun.

"The man who kills kids."

Her eyes sparked as she blinked again, scraping flint. Then she spread her arms and touched her fingertips together, enclosing an unseen shape.

"A round place," said Danny Apple.

Her eyes went up and up.

"A tall place," said Buffalo Bob.

"Is that where he lives?"

She nodded.

"Is he there now?"

Again she nodded.

"What about Chris? Is he there?"

No.

"Is he—is he alive?"

She made no movement.

243

"She doesn't know."

"What does the man look like, the man who took him?"

She drew them close on the platform, the wino, the freak and the jockey, holding them together to form one shape.

"He's big."

"He's strong."

She pointed at the sky, dropped her arm quickly and made a cutting motion from ear to ear across her throat.

"He has a blade."

"Then you've got to help us," David said, "before it's too late."

She backed away.

"She says she can't do that."

Then something hit the pavement at the mouth of the alley, struck a drainpipe, rang on the roof vents and the steel door, falling between the buildings. It was all around them, everywhere at once. The rain.

ʎ

On their way back up the footpath, Leanne asked, "Why do you call him the Professor?"

"Barton?" said the thin man with the ponytail. "He used to teach at the University of the Pacific. One day some men in gray suits came around. After that, no one would hire him. This is where he ended up."

"What about you?"

"I went with him. He's my old man."

"I thought so." She considered the shape of his head, the eyes. "But why here? I don't mean to be rude . . ." She lowered her voice so the others, two men who were built like out-of-shape wrestlers, would not hear. "You are living in a garbage dump, aren't you?"

"There was no place else to go."

"But surely . . ."

"There used to be a support system, if you wanted to drop out. Not anymore."

I don't get it, she thought.

"But *why*?"

"Everybody has his own reasons. Some of us can't live by rules we didn't make."

"Nobody likes rules," she said, "but you've got to have order, don't you?"

"That's why we have the Articles."

"What are they?"

"I'll tell you about them sometime, if you really want to know."

It must be something important, she thought, for people to give up indoor plumbing, telephones, supermarkets, all the myriad advantages of civilization.

"I guess I just don't get it."

"Take a look around," he said, meaning more than the chaparral between the hills. "Don't you ever wonder what happened to our generation? The best and the brightest, all the things they were going to do . . . Now they're driving cabs, washing dishes, pumping gas. There's a generation, a whole nation that disappeared, millions of them. They're still here, but they're invisible. What they had to offer, it's all wasted. At least in Box City, they're honest about it. It's the only place I've ever been where no one bothers to lie."

"And you think this isn't a waste?" Get him cleaned up, she thought, cut his hair, put him in a nice suit, nothing fancy, say from C&R, and who knows what he couldn't do? He'd make quite a lawyer. Just listen to that closing argument.

"It's a start," he said.

"What does *that* mean?"

"Think about it. If some of those millions out there decide to quit one day, walk off the job and never go back, there may be a lot more Box Cities." For some reason the idea cheered him. "If that happens, everything will stop. Who's going to keep things running? Who's going to shovel shit and clean up other people's messes for them? They'll have to start doing it for themselves—which won't last long. Then maybe there won't be any more shit to shovel." He heard himself ranting and stopped self-consciously. "Anyway, it's a thought. Ask Barton. He's the intellectual."

She tried to muster an argument. "It doesn't seem very safe." She pictured a band of outlaw bikers swooping down on the landfill and trashing it, like Indians around a camp, or the cavalry around an Indian village. "What do you do about people who don't follow your Articles? Like the one who walked in last night and killed the children's pet? He didn't belong to your group, and look what happened."

"He only belongs to himself. That's why he's dangerous."

"But what *about* him, and others like him?"

"That's why we have to move on. The only mistake Barton made was not getting far enough away from civilization."

He's a hopeless romantic, she thought. Rousseau and all that. It can't work. Civilization will follow wherever you go, like crabgrass. You'll never get far enough away from it, unless the real cities start to die off. Which isn't likely. Still, she had to admit that the idea was not completely without appeal for her, in a wacky sort of way. Postindustrialism, she thought. She'd heard the term on *MacNeil/Lehrer*, but it hadn't meant anything till now. The first wobbly steps for those who get an impossible idea in their heads and can't let go of it. They're brave, and very, very foolish.

"I hope you're not trying to recruit me," she said.

"Would I do that?" he said, and smiled his famous smile.

"Oh . . . !"

"What's wrong?"

"Listen!"

He motioned for the other men to stop.

"Don't tell me they have snakes around here," she said. "Please don't tell me that . . . !"

There was a hissing and a tapping, as though insects too small to see were walking on the leaves, a distant warning system for the approach of something evil. The sound grew, filling the ravine and the entire basin, magnified by the hills, as raindrops began to fall around them.

"We better get a move on, Peter," said one of the men. "Look at that sky."

It was stony now, with a black tumorous mass behind it, moving in from the coast, passing over the city, coming fast.

"Hold on," said the other man. "She doesn't need us, after all . . ."

Ahead, where the footpath ended and started, someone was moving by the wrecked Mustang. She recognized the suit. On the access road above, another car was parked near hers, a portable red light revolving on the roof.

God only knew what had brought the Chief up here.

The thin man held out his hand. "Good luck to you."

"Thank you," she said. "I don't even know your name. What was it he called you?"

"It doesn't matter. I don't know yours, either."

As the rain came down her face was washed slick as a baby's skin, and her hands, the water seeping into the bandage on her palm, into the cut, so that it bled with the water, and stung with the opening of it and the exchange of oxygen between the blood flowing in her body and the rest of the world.

She looked at the pain and felt the wonder of it there, in her hand.

He had lowered his arm. It was too late to return the gesture.

"Are you all right? Your hand . . ."

"It's nothing."

"You sure?"

"Yes. I'm sure."

"Well, good-bye, then."

"Good-bye."

Her hair was stringy and curling, the mascara trickling from her lashes into her eyes. She didn't want him to remember her this way. It was time to go.

When she got up to the road she looked back once, but he was gone.

The darkness had not yet come this far.

From the front, McKenzie Hall could have been a junior high school, a public utility, a retirement home. Not until they were past Admissions & Holding did Martin notice the chickenwire glass, and the oversized keyrings such as those carried by used car dealers or nightwatchmen that dangled from the belts of every employee.

Lissa bypassed the timeclock and unlocked the door to a covered walkway.

"That's Tiger Cottage," she told him, meaning the low buildings across the courtyard. "And the Chipmunks, Bears, Foxes . . . I work in Lions, Junior and Senior Girls."

When he didn't say anything, she stopped walking.

"I still say you should be home."

What home? he thought.

"I have to see if he's here."

"He's not, according to the roster, and I'm sure the police have checked by now."

"Then one of your kids may know who he is."

"Jack, you ought to be in bed. You don't look so good."

Did she mean his clothes? They fit, but only barely. When the time had come for him to sneak out of the hospital with Lissa, after the young Deputy took his finished sketch and left, clothing was the main problem. His shirt and trousers were dry, but torn and covered with mud. Another closet held what the man in the other bed, the one behind the curtain, had worn at check-in: a forty-year-old brown tweed suit that smelled of mothballs, a white cotton twill shirt, a wide

251

necktie and a pair of Florsheim wingtips. Martin took the shirt and slacks and coat, kept his own shoes, such as they were, and left what cash he had, twenty-three dollars and some change. It was hardly fair, but the sallow old fellow smiled around his feeding tubes, waving him away. It might have meant that he hated the suit and was glad to be rid of it at any price. Or that he didn't expect to be needing it again.

"Just tell me where to start."

She saw there was no dissuading him. "Well, we could try Junior Boys. Second lunch is almost over."

The atmosphere in the cafeteria suggested canned spaghetti and Wonder Bread. The Senior Boys were slugging down purple Kool-Aid and telling dirty jokes in the corner by the steam table, while the Juniors still sat at long wooden tables, hunkered over their ice-cream bowls with spoons in their fists, legs tucked securely under the benches.

A counselor in a denim workshirt and round glasses got up as soon as she came in the door.

"Hey, Leesa," he said with an affected drawl. "What're you doing here?"

"Bill, would you do something for me?"

"What did you do, switch shifts?"

"No, I'm off today . . ."

"Can't stay away, huh?"

"Bill, will you—?"

A bell rang jarringly, as if an alarm clock were embedded in the walls. The Senior Boys swung their legs around and swaggered up.

"Tell them to wait," Lissa said.

"You got it."

He plugged his mouth with a silver whistle and blew. It was enough to cause physical pain to Martin's eardrums. Then Bill spat out the whistle and let it hang from the lanyard around his neck, like a pacifier on a string.

"Did I say dismissed?" he shouted.

"No-o-o . . ." said the Senior Boys.

The Junior Boys stayed where they were, cowed as dogs ready for a whipping.

"No, *sir*!" said Bill.

"No, sir . . ."

He held his chin high, showing off for Lissa.

"Ask them if they know this boy." She handed him a copy of the poster with Christopher's picture.

"Who is he?"

"Bill, please . . ."

"Do any of you—Manny, I'm talking! Eyes front!"

253

"I don't know nothing, okay?" said a homeboy in khakis and a crew-neck T-shirt. "Can we go? I gotta take a dump real bad! Okay?"

His friends, some in Pendleton shirts hanging open except for the top two buttons, snickered and rocked back and forth.

"Okay, *Mr. Soon.* Manny, you're on KP."

The homeboy groaned.

"Give it to me," said Lissa. She took the paper and went to the end of the benches, ignoring the Seniors.

"Hi. I'm Miss Shelby, from Lion Cottage."

The Junior Boys recognized her.

"Let's play a game, all right?"

They relaxed slightly.

"Whoever can tell me who this boy is will win fifty points on the Star Chart, how's that?"

One little boy raised his hand. "What's his name?"

"That's what you have to tell *me.* Have you ever seen him?"

"Was he bad?"

"No, he's a very, very good boy. That's why I think you know him. Don't you? Come on, now."

A child with a gold front tooth said, "He's on Nickelodeon."

"No, I'm afraid that's not right. He does sort of look like him, though, doesn't he?"

"Chris," said a voice.

Martin moved up to see who it was. "There, in back," he told her.

Then one of the senior boys loaded a tape player. Music flooded the room.

"Jamel!" shouted Bill. "Put that away! This isn't the dayroom!"

"Let them go," said Lissa. "I'm trying to . . ."

"Table One, line up!"

Lissa turned back to the benches. "Who said that?"

The little boys didn't make a sound.

"Somebody has the right answer," she said. "I heard it."

Nobody said anything as Bill marched the older boys outside.

"Who's he?" asked the one with the gold tooth.

"This is my friend Jack. He's an artist—he drew this picture. Can you all see it? Now who said 'Chris'?"

A tentative hand went up.

"Jeffrey Batters? Your sister is in Lions, isn't she?"

"Yeah . . ."

"Well, congratulations, Jeffrey! You just

255

won fifty points on the board. You can use that for extra play, or TV time, or anything you want. Tell Mr. Soon I said so. Now who knows where Christopher lives?"

"He doesn't live nowhere," said Jeffrey.

"Anywhere," corrected Lissa. "He doesn't live . . ."

Bill Soon reappeared at the door. "I can take them back to their unit now."

"In a minute, Bill . . . Jeffrey, why do you say he doesn't live anywhere?"

"Because he lives in the alley."

"You mean he's a homeless person, a homeless little boy. Is that right?"

"Yeah. I saw him lots of times. He sleeps there, too."

"And what alley is that?"

The boy shrugged.

"I knew it," Martin said to her. "That's why he showed up at the Cove. It was where he used to live. He didn't know where else to go."

"Do I win, Miss Shelby?"

"Yes, Jeffrey. You get fifty *more* points if you know which alley."

"All of them."

Martin's eyes flickered, a wave of tiredness passing through him as she continued.

"And does Christopher have a mother and father?"

Exaggerated shrugs.

Outside, somewhere beyond the courtyard, there was a loud boom.

"What's that, Miss Shelby?"

"It's only thunder," she explained. Still, she had been jolted. "You all know what that is. You're not afraid of thunder, are you?"

"No-o-o . . ."

Another white phosphor flash ignited the sky. Someone was coming this way across the courtyard, an overexposed background behind his blacked-in head. Then he was at the doorway. The sky grew quite dark.

"It's time for second bell, Lees," said Bill impatiently.

"Right. Come on, boys, line up. Stay with Mr. Soon."

"Do I get points, too?"

"Yes, you all get points, how about that?"

The thunder hit a few seconds closer this time. The boys moved jerkily, their eyes dilated, hyperalert.

"Will you go with us, Miss Shelby?"

"Yes, of course. Come on, Tigers . . ."

She hustled them out and lined them up on the covered walkway.

"Aren't you going to introduce us, Lissa?" said Bill as they walked the boys to the unit.

"What?"

"Your . . . friend."

"Oh, I'm sorry, this is Mr. Martin. He— he's thinking of coming to work for us."

"The pay's lousy, the food's government surplus, and you never get enough sleep, the way they keep changing the schedule around," Bill said discouragingly. "Plus the kids are a pain in the ass. They never leave you alone."

"They need us," said Lissa. "They're starved for attention. For now, we're all they've got. We have to be mothers, fathers, teachers . . ."

"Yeah, on a civil service salary!"

"There are other benefits. We get to see them grow, find out who they are, learn to cope . . . I had a girl who ate with her hands and didn't know how to dress herself. By the time we found her a placement . . ."

The patch of open sky flashed again, then turned charcoal. A second later the thunder hit. The storm was closing the gap. Small faces appeared at the windows of Lion Cottage, between crayon drawings of stick people with big hands and stretched limbs. A little girl in a pink sweatshirt screamed and ran outside, as the first raindrops hit.

Martin broke from the walkway and went for her. She only screamed louder and dodged him, running farther from the unit.

"Wait," Lissa called to him. "That's Ruthie J. . . . I'll get her!"

The rain came faster, pelting the courtyard. Drops as large as gobs of paint spattered the girl's dress and stained it with dark splotches, as if she were bleeding from within. Lissa caught her around the waist and lifted her off her feet, then carried her under the awning. When Martin got to them, Ruthie was hysterical. Across the way, the line of junior boys watched with fascination and dismay, witnesses to an accident in progress.

"She's acting-out," said Lissa. "Help me get her inside. . . ."

Martin held her kicking legs through the dayroom of the Junior Girls' wing, past a jury of faces with trembling lips and moist eyes. Lissa cradled Ruthie on the sofa and restrained her.

Another counselor, Lucy Rodriguez, hurried out of the staff bathroom, trailing a wisp of cigarette smoke from her hair.

"Girls, go to your rooms. Lissa, is that you? I'll call the Infirmary."

"No, we're fine, Lucy. Get me a towel."

They dried Ruthie as Lissa rocked her on her lap, whispering words in her ear, kissing her hair, holding her till she stopped fighting.

Lucy said, "Here, I'll put her to bed."

"That's not necessary. Is it, Ruthie? We'll just sit here and get acquainted. I'm Lissa, and this is my new friend, Ruthie. She's special." To Lucy she said, "I can take it from here. She's on my Monday caseload. We may as well start now."

"How about some rainy-day activities?" Lucy said to the assembled group. "Seven-Up, Hangman . . . ?"

All eyes were on Lissa. The outburst had triggered a release of emotion in the other girls, and now they stood close around the sofa to see how it would resolve. Ruthie was one of them, and it was important that the episode have closure. Lissa understood that. It came from something more than training. Martin was impressed.

"Well," said Lucy, "if you don't need me for a few minutes, I *was* on my break . . ."

"Go ahead, Lucy. I have to talk to Ruthie, anyway."

"Thanks, Lees. I'm glad you were here."

"So am I."

The drops blew in waves against the bungalow, making a drumhead of the flat roof. Martin felt the pressure building inside the room as the tempo increased. The children felt it, too. The sound of the rain through the low ceiling made them nervous, even as Ruthie calmed down enough to suck her thumb.

Martin sat on his end of the sofa.

"Do any of you know about the Man With No Face?"

Lissa's eyes nailed him. "Don't. Not now."

He held his hand up, fending her off. "We have to."

"Listen to me. This isn't the right time."

"What is? I'm sorry, but time is running out."

He took in the girls' faces, some in process, half-formed, incipient young women already, others hardly more than babies, with fatted cheeks and button noses, but all so small, so weak, so vulnerable. It tore his heart to question them. He saw eyes that were ready to leak tears at his next word, a sure sign that they knew something. He had to go on.

"Who is he?"

261

"He's the bad man," said one girl.

Thunder resounded as rain battered the roof full force, jumping in the courtyard, pouring over the panes. Lissa covered Ruthie's ears and said, "Shh, shh, don't listen," holding her close, protecting her.

"I'm going to find the bad man," said Martin, "so he can't hurt anyone again. But first I have to know where he is."

"He's in the attic," said another girl.

"He hides under the stairs."

"He comes in your room when you're sleeping."

"He killed my dog . . ."

"Where?" said Martin. "Where is he?"

Ruthie sat up, her face as neutral as a sleepwalker's. "He finds you when you play out at nighttime," she said calmly. "He takes you to the castle. He locks the door, and then he takes you up in the mountains and buries you in the ground. And you can't get out. And nobody can find you. *Never.* He did that to my friend. I saw him."

"What did you see?"

"I saw where he went. He chased me, and I falled down. He couldn't find me. I told my daddy. He said it was a scary dream. But Roseanna, she never came back."

One of the little girls started to cry.

"Where is this castle?"

"In the mountains, at the beach."

"Stop it, Jack. She's fantasizing. She's—"

"How do you know?"

"I know because there are no castles around here!"

"It could be a house."

"There are no houses that are both in the mountains *and* at the beach."

"Yes, there are. Tell me about the house, Ruthie. The castle."

"It's round. It has glass, and roses, and bird flowers. They have movies there. Kids like to go. But they never come home."

"That's it."

"That's *what*? Jack, look at them," Lissa said over the drilling rain. "They're frightened. This has got to stop . . ."

"The Roundhouse," said Jack.

"The what?"

Martin kissed Ruthie on the forehead.

"Take a nap now, honey," he said. "And when you wake up, the bad man will be gone, I promise. He's never coming back."

He held out his hand to Lissa.

"Give me your keys," he said.

Part Five
The Roundhouse

13.

Sitting in the Chief's car, Leanne wondered how long the rain would last. It descended in a torrent over the windshield. The Deputies who dragged the body up from the ravine had legs made of gelatin and putty faces.

The Chief hung up his CB microphone. "At least I got to this one before the boys from Santa Mara."

"Those aren't your men?" she asked.

"The Sheriff's. They've wanted to take over since this business started."

"When did it? There were others, before Friday, I know that. How many?"

He rubbed his eyes. "Seven, that we know about," he said in a defeated voice.

How could that be? Leanne remembered

reading about one, perhaps two other children before Friday. But not seven.

"They weren't all reported, then."

"No, ma'am, they weren't. When it started again last summer, the City Council got worried about the tourists—it almost killed the town, before. And I went along with it, oh, didn't I? to keep it out of the papers . . . but now it's too late for that. Too late."

"What do you mean, 'again'?"

"How long did you say you've lived here?"

"Six years."

He flexed his gloved hands on the wheel, exercising them, trying to pump up the strength he would need.

"The first time was about eight years ago. A string of missing children, up and down the area. We found one, and parts of some others. Someone was killing them, burying the bodies. He must have buried them deep. We never found them all.

"Then it stopped, and we figured it was over. The Council was glad to hear that. So Shadow Bay got to be *the* place again. Good schools, housing, weather . . . until the last few years. The fog came in, like a cloud over the town. This time it lasted. Now that the killing has started again, everybody will know how much more there is to it. . . ."

The rope over the cliff edge tightened and the Deputies pulled like primitive fishermen, backs straining. A body bag came into view.

"I'll get one of my men to follow you down."

"That's not necessary."

"The road might wash out. It's been a long time since we had a rain like this."

He was right, as far as she could remember. The statewide drought had been in effect here, too. Now rain like buckshot pelted the top of the car, melting over the windows, down into the inner workings of the door, where the window motors and lock mechanisms were.

"What were you doing up here, Mrs. Martin?" he asked without any real interest.

"I don't know. Honestly, I don't. I took a wrong turn, and then I thought I could find my way back."

It was an unlikely story. She didn't expect the Chief to believe her.

"What about you?" she said.

He turned his head in the liquid light and spoke to her chin, her hair, the headrest, anything but her eyes.

"It was what you said, about the hills. It occurred to me that you might have wanted to tell me something. Do you?"

"No. I don't know what I meant. It was a —a dream I had."

"Well, your dream came true, didn't it?"

A young policeman, one of the Chief's, knocked on the window. His mouth opened and closed like a fish. Pennington let the glass down an inch.

"Should I go with the ambulance, Chief?"

"No need, Tommy. You go and see that they didn't miss anything up on top, before it gets washed away."

"Yes, sir." The policeman saw Leanne across the front seat and tipped his hat. Rainwater slopped off the brim and ran into the car through the opening at the top of the window.

"And Tommy?"

"Yes, Chief?"

"Any sign of Sheriff Pritchard yet?"

"No, sir."

"That's all." The Chief closed the window. "He'll be here soon enough," he said to her. "Then there'll be hell to pay."

"What's up on top?" she said. He must mean the top of the hill, she thought.

"The other half of that little girl's body."

"No!" She was dumbfounded. "You mean the one from the beach?"

"It looks that way. There were tooth

marks, but not from any shark. She was buried up there in one piece. Animals found the grave, dug her up, got to chewing . . . Half washed down with the river, into the old drain that empties by the Point. That was why your husband found her on the beach. The top half, that is. My guess is that's how the other one, the one we found on Friday, got into the city sewer system. It was all in one piece, and it was too big."

"How did you know where to look?"

"A boy came into the station this morning. Said he and some friends of his saw something up there the other night, when there was a full moon. He was right. Funny thing is, I was coming up here anyway, after you put it in my mind."

"I didn't know anything about that. Believe me. Not anything."

"And you didn't know anything about this one, either."

"I didn't. I—I was just . . ."

"You took a wrong turn. Like in your dream."

The Chief rubbed his eyes harder, as if he had seen too much and wished to erase the memory. He was older now, with creases in the shape of X's on the back of his neck, and the first signs of liver spots.

"I know it sounds crazy," she said. "I saw the car as I was driving down to the coast highway. I went to get help."

"And did you find it?"

"No." Does he know about the Box People? she wondered. He must. But it would be better not to involve them, if possible.

"Just as well. There's a tribe of hippies not far from here. They're harmless, but I guess someone will have to question them now."

"They don't know anything."

"No?"

Too late; he had caught her.

"No."

"You're sure about that."

"I'm sure. They said . . ."

"What did they say?"

"They said—he's come back."

"They were right about that much."

The Chief unfurled a handkerchief like a flag of surrender and wiped his nose.

"I'd advise you, Mrs. Martin, to go down that road now, to wherever you were going. The Sheriff's boys will already have a make on the car in the ravine. When Pritchard gets here, he'll know all about the man, and that he lived in the Cove. As does your husband. And that they were the best of friends. He'll conduct his own investigation. In a few more

272

minutes, the case will be out of my hands. As well it should be."

"You did all you could, I'm sure."

"Did I?" His voice cracked and he cleared his throat. "I could have stopped it years ago. I should never have listened to them . . ."

Them? she thought. Who? The City Council? The Mayor? Had the Chief known something and not acted on it?

They sat that way for another minute, avoiding each other's eyes. She could not be sure why the Chief looked so broken, though she suspected that it had to do with something more than dead children, something even closer to home, something that he thought had been buried and now was not.

$$\bigwedge$$

Lay four caskets side by side. Paint them black, and stack them one on top of the other. Viewed from either end, they will form a vertical rectangle approximately thirty inches wide and six feet tall, roughly the size of an open grave.

Or a doorway, open on darkness . . .

There was only one tall, round structure in Shadow Bay.

The water tower.

Beneath the tower was a shed, housing the pipes and meters and valves that distributed water to the homes and businesses of the city. The shed was kept closed between inspections, with a heavy-duty padlock that could not be sawed off or jimmied. That latch was old, the screws that held it in place rusted through, but this was of no great concern to the Santa Mara County Water Department. Who would bother to break into such a structure, and what damage could anyone do, without the special wrenches and tools required to divert the flow through such massive pipes?

The latch itself, however, presented no challenge to anyone determined to find refuge from the elements.

The boys saw this as soon as they got within fifty feet of it. The shed was already open, the latch dangling free. Rain slashed across the doorway, a vertical rectangle dark as the entrance to a tomb.

"He's in there," said David.

Now the others, who had behaved so recklessly on the way, stayed close together in the driest spot they could find, behind one of the

274

tower's supports. The tank at the top was lost in mist, a giant primordium extending into a black-veined sky, but it provided some slight protection for a small patch of ground below, like an umbrella raised into the storm by four iron arms.

"What if we're too late?" said Kevin. His jacket was soaked and his ears were dripping, and he looked over his shoulder at the city, where lights already beckoned from the windows of homes at the edge of the residential section, as if ready to bolt.

"How do we know he's even got him in there?" said Jamie.

"If he does, we get him out," said David. "If he doesn't . . ."

"Yeah," said Robby, "if he doesn't, then we kick ass."

"How do we do *that*?" said Kevin. "Are *you* gonna do it?"

David said, "He's got to be stopped."

Nobody argued with him.

"Well," said Jamie, "whatever we're gonna do, we better do it now, 'cause I'm sure not goin' in there after it's dark."

"Let's go," said David. "Jamie, you go around the side. Kev, you go to the back . . ."

"What do you want *me* to do?" said Robby.

He was having a hard time holding himself back, like a pit bull on a short leash.

"You cover me."

For a moment nobody moved. What they were about to do settled over them, falling out of a heavy sky with the weight of reality.

"Nobody's in there," said Kevin.

"It's empty," said Jamie.

Thunder cracked, and then lightning flashed, throwing the shed and its slant roof into stark relief under the tilted legs of the tower. Then water poured down the legs, as though the tank had split open, puddling in front of the doorway. The door slapped wide, opening and shutting, opening and shutting in the rising wind, as the full fury of the storm was released.

Ready or not, here I come.

"I have to know," said David, and ran for the door.

When he was halfway there, another flash of lightning. This time something definitely moved inside the shed, strobing in black-and-white between the humped pipes. Then the doorway was dark again.

David stopped in front of the door, where segmented earthworms thrashed and drowned in two inches of runny-brown water, flopping over the threshold, leaving a trail of slime.

"Chris?" he said, as runoff from the roof doused his head.

A sound like wind chimes came from inside.

"Come on out, if you're there."

To his right, Jamie ran along the side of the shed. To his left, Kevin ducked around the back.

"Chris, if you can hear me . . ."

Again the chimes.

The door creaked, swinging free. David flattened against it and looked around for a weapon. Just inside, a Coke bottle sparkled.

"I'm coming in."

He extended his foot, made contact with the bottle. It spun on its side like a compass. He kicked again, nudging the bottle over a knot of slippery worms. Then he bent his knees and reached for it, as something came down hard on the back of his hand, pinning him to the boards.

He used his other hand to try to free himself, and grasped a boot.

Lightning flashed.

He looked up and up, and saw a man in a long black coat looming over him. The man was standing on David's fingers.

277

As the lightning ended, David grabbed the bottle and swung it against the shin. The glass broke and the boot lifted, releasing him. Then the boot kicked and caught him square in the face. He fell back, then sprang to his feet and jabbed with the broken bottle. He connected. There was a grunt. Thunder shook the shed, rattling the chimes. When the next flash came he saw the man doubled over, boots sliding on the worms, holding his nose and dripping blood into a crate of empty bottles. David grabbed another one out of the crate and smashed it into the man's head.

"You little bastard, I'll kill you!"

At the sound of the voice, the other boys ran in the open door. They couldn't see anything at all till the lightning came again. At the next flash Jamie kicked as hard as he could, as Kevin picked up the case of tinkling bottles and brought it down on the man's back. Then darkness. Then another flash, to show Robby with two bottles in his hands, swinging wildly. The bottles shattered as the lights went out again. At the next flash, Robby was jabbing at the doubled-over figure and blood was spurting onto the walls and ceiling, the pipes and valves, each drop frozen in time, like red dotted lines on the air. The man squealed like a stuck pig. The thunder drowned out the sound. With each irregular flash, Robby was lunging with the broken bottle, spearing the beast between the shoulder blades, hacking away at the artery on its neck, going for its ears and its eyes and its tongue, all the while cursing in a high-pitched, hysterical girl's voice, *"Die, you motherfucker, die!"* and the blood everywhere, transforming the shed into an abattoir. Then David and Jamie and Kevin were dragging their friend outside, holding his wrists, making him drop what was left of the bottles, as the rain came down and washed them all in the blood.

"Never hit me again, you son of a bitch, never! I'll kill you first! I'll cut off your balls! I'll—"

"Who, Robby? Who are you talking about? Robby . . ."

"It's over . . ."

"Over!"

Robby blinked.

"Hi, Davy," he said. "Did we do it? Did we get him?"

David left them and walked back and stood waiting for the lightning to flash again. It took a long time. The rain hissed down

279

inside and outside the shed. His friends filled the doorway and waited with him. When it finally came it was fast, like a low-wattage lightbulb shorting out, and only a weak flicker spread across the floor, sawtoothed by the shadows of their heads. It was enough to show the crumpled body of a bum, the wild, wet hair, the flayed skin of the face, the eye against the boards, the widening ruby pool by the head and the steaming piss flowing out past the long coat. He did not look so tall now. He was only a man.

"We got someone," said David.

"Is—is he the one?"

A terrible silence fell over them.

"He better be."

"But it looks like Old John. You know, the wino . . . ?"

"That's not Old John."

"No, it can't be. Old John never hurt anybody. It's—*him*."

"Yeah."

"Sure."

"Is he dead?"

"Dead . . ."

"Well, then . . . what do we do now?"

"We go home."

They were to the first signal at the end of

Main Street before someone remembered about Chris.

Leanne drove back down from the hills with white knuckles. She might as well have been driving blind. The blade on her windshield wiper was broken, two loose flaps of rubber squeaking and chattering as dollops of rain smacked into the glass like water balloons. It grew dark out, too dark for this time of day, as if the town below lay in the path of a solar eclipse. She inched along at five miles an hour and wondered, How long can it last?

A torrent fell out of the sky, so quickly and with such abundance that the ground could not hold it. The surface of the unpaved road rippled and moved away from her feeble headlights. In the rearview mirror she saw the hillside swelling, extruding mud to cover the tire tracks winding out behind her. She cranked her window open, stuck her head out and held her wheels as far away as possible from the edge of the ravine. Then the other side of the car scraped the hill, tearing at the dead roots and breaking a layer of shale into jagged rocks that tumbled ahead, racing her to the bottom. As the eyes of the city came into view she eased up on the brakes, and a loose chunk of granite hit the top of the car.

She looked up, expecting to see a hole. There was a bulge in the headliner, as though a fat slug had crawled in between the metal and the fabric. Fortunately it was not moving, though the domelight now hung at a severe angle, ready to drop onto her shoulder or into her hair.

She toed the accelerator and moved forward again, but not before several more granite chunks the size of golf balls struck the hood and windshield. One of the rocks chipped the safety glass and a network of fine cracks spread out from the point of impact, an instant spiderweb radiating across the rectangle of her vision. She held her foot down and spun off the access road, heading for the start of the residential section.

There seemed to be a flurry of activity within some of the houses, with silhouettes shuffling back and forth behind the curtains and front doors cracking open at the sound of her passing. At the end of Rosewood Avenue a couple came out onto the porch and waved vigorously at her, but the noise of the rainfall on her car, like shelled peas dropped into an empty bucket, made it impossible for her to hear what they were saying.

The signal at the end of Main and the headlights coming toward her melted into one another, as the boundaries between light and darkness that had defined the town dissolved before her eyes. She passed four boys on foot. Without raincoats they were soaked to the skin, yet they did not appear to be in any hurry, trudging grimly to or from some secret ritual that disapproving adults would never know about. She thought of offering them a ride. When she slowed by the curb not one of them acknowledged her. She drove on.

I wonder what's happened to the old woman? she thought.

Where did the homeless go at times like this? There can't be that many covered doorways. She realized that she had no idea how many such people there were in Shadow Bay, though she suspected there were quite a few. They were the invisible underclass that the majority did not like to think about. Wasn't there something that could be done to help them? Simple shelter, hot meals, perhaps in the church, even the high school auditorium, at least whenever the weather got this bad. Some must have children; what happens to them? You can't expect babies to eat spoiled hamburgers from garbage cans and sleep in shopping carts—they might drown. Or do they grow up wild, on their own, like feral animals?

If they head for the hills, she thought, they can always join the Box People.

What a prospect! No education, no hope for the future . . . They had seemed happy enough. That was because they didn't know, had never known anything better. Give them careful baths, real beds and rooms of their own, toys, school clothes, video games, teach them to comb their hair and grow up and get jobs, and they'll be all right. We'll all be all right. Won't we?

The one with the ponytail, and his father, they couldn't be right. An army of dropouts, turning tail and running for the hills, growing into some kind of alien nation cut off from the real world . . . It could get to be a problem.

They only wanted to be left alone, they said. But to do what? How, for that matter, did they get their food? She imagined some of them sneaking down in the night, bartering for supplies at the back doors of restaurants. Some might not be so honorable. Some might let themselves into houses, kitchens, refrigerators, cupboards, living off the rest of us. They're envious. We have what they want, and that's dangerous. Unless they really don't want it. And now they have to move on, as if they're more afraid of us than we are of them.

What if more people decide to join them, walk off the job and never come back, as he had predicted? He had spoken as if he believed it would be the start of a new world. She tried now to imagine it. The only image that came to mind was of eyes, millions of them, billions, like stars, mountains of eyes gathering in packs around the rim of the world, gazing down hungrily. It must be how the whites in Africa feel, she thought. A minority, when you take the whole population into consideration. And some, if what he had said was true, smarter and more talented than those who were left behind. That part was not easy to believe, though he sounded very sure of himself. The only way to survive in that case would be to join them. She did not want to consider the possibility, and tried to put it out of her mind.

Her thoughts went on in that vein awhile longer, until she was brought up short at a signal. She had the uneasy experience of having driven somewhere unconsciously, without noting or remembering how she had gotten here. How long had she been tuned out?

An ambulance from the hospital passed her, headed for the access road. She pulled over to the side of the street and waited. When the siren faded, she looked ahead in case any more red lights might be coming. There were none, but she did see something in the sky, moving this way, supported by a pillar of white light.

It was too low to be an airplane. As it drew closer she saw that it was a helicopter, shining a beacon on the streets and buildings below. It passed over and for an instant her car was bathed in the glow of a bright noonday sun. Then it was behind her, aiming its searchlight at the hills.

That must be Sheriff Pritchard, she thought. From Santa Mara. An impressive entrance.

She put her hands back on the steering wheel and touched the gas pedal.

And hit the brake.

A man was standing there.

"Oh! God, you scared me . . ."

He couldn't hear her through the windshield, even if it was cracked. Where had he come from? He had materialized out of the rain, one of the shadows from between the buildings, a shadow with legs, or feet at least, a few inches below the long coat. He had his collar up and his head down so she couldn't see his face.

He was directly in front of her car, and made no move to get out of the way.

He must know I'm here, unless he's blind.

Her low beams bounced off the middle of his coat between where the waist and knees would have been, lending a gloss to the wet fabric so that it resembled the fur of a panther caught out in the storm. He had no hat, at least she didn't think he did, only a mat of black hair.

She shifted into Park and opened her door.

"Can I help you?" she said. "Are you . . . ?"

He took a step to the side, then moved purposefully along her car, brushing against it. She heard what she thought was the long scratching of a button against the paint, louder as she sat back down and closed her door. Or was it fingernails? If it is he must be blind, feeling his way. She slid across the seat and unlocked the passenger door.

Oh well, she thought, it's an old car.

As the door opened, she heard a sizzle and a pop. Overhead, the domelight had gone on and immediately shorted out. Drops of water clung to the opaque lamp housing. That meant the top of her car had been punctured, after all, and water was leaking in. She felt despair, thinking what that would cost to repair.

"I'm only going as far as the beach," she said, "but if you need a lift, I suppose . . ."

Where was his cane, if he was blind? Too late; he was inside.

She recoiled at the smell that got in with him. It was as bad as a sheep ready for dipping. Uh-oh, she thought, I hope he's not one of the homeless. Then she was ashamed at her reaction. If he is, then charity begins at home. They need to get from place to place just like anyone else. Still, she had never had one in her car before. A part of her, however, hoped that it was only the usual reek of wet wool that she was smelling.

She shifted up to Drive and started off.

"Isn't this rain terrible? I've never seen anything like it. They said on the news that a storm was coming, but I never . . ."

She was talking too fast, out of sheer nervousness. It was because he hadn't spoken. She tried to get a better look at him without turning her head. All she saw was the heavy coat dripping water onto the floor. Her car

seat would swell up like a sponge and de-
velop mildew unless she could manage to air
it out. A hairdryer?

"I can't stand to see people walking in the
rain," she said. "It's—it's dangerous."

He did not answer.

The diner and self-serve gas station slid by
outside, and eventually the police station and
the hospital. Farther ahead were the coastal
residence streets and then the sea itself; a
brief wedge of it showed like a spilled cupful
of black pearls at the very end of Main.

"Where . . . ?" There was a frog in her
throat. She swallowed with some effort and
tried again. "Where would you like to be
dropped?"

She didn't feel well. Her hair was sopping
again, drenching her collar; the skin of her
neck was cold and damp. If she wasn't careful she'd end up with a sore throat, or worse.
She was growing distinctly uneasy. In her
mirror she saw a police car leave the station,
but it was going in the opposite direction.

As she watched the taillights getting
smaller, the mirror clouded over with condensation. The windows were steaming up,
too. It was the wet coat, the breath of their
talking—of her talking. She flipped on the
heater and defroster. The blast of air was

witheringly cold on her legs and hands. She turned it off. Another traffic light came into view, switching too quickly from yellow to red. She watched a drop of water trickle down from the top of her windshield, to join other drops that had penetrated the glass at the center of the spiderweb. The storm was inside as well. She was more vulnerable than she had known, with only a thin manufactured shell to protect her, a shell that might crack at any time, as apparently it already had.

"I said, where—?"

She took her right hand off the wheel and reached for the man's shoulder to make sure that he was all right and that he had heard her, to touch him.

Click.

And something ice cold was at her throat, supporting her chin on its point, so swiftly that she could not have known what was coming.

14.

For most cars on the coast highway, the turnoff to Eden Cove was a break in the foliage, nothing more; there were no signs, and if you did not know exactly where to look you would pass it by without a second thought.

Martin had started off from the Hall, but before he got a mile away his foot was so cold and numb he could not be sure how hard he was riding the gas pedal. That and the condition of Lissa's car, with the driver's door caved in and the window broken so that the rain blew in as if it were a convertible with a slashed top, made it impossible for him to get up any speed. When she withheld the keys unless he included her, he could not refuse, and the argument became academic anyway as soon as she got to the car before him. When the Datsun threatened to stall because of his lead-footed technique she demanded that he let her take over, but he kept going, the bashed frame carrying them along at a bent, misaligned angle, like a crab on wheels. Now he wished he had listened to her, not because she was so angry and so frightened as much as the way his leg was cramping up, and the ache from the water and wind blowing into his ear. Even with the wipers on high the trees were confusingly similar through the rain, so he unlocked his knee with one hand and manually lifted his foot off the gas, coasting along until he was going slowly enough to be absolutely sure about the opening and the dark driveway.

Wet quartz cracked and rolled under the tires like the gravel at the bottom of a tide-pool, washed and rounded by flowing water. The water funneled ahead of the car, past the gatehouse to the parking lot, where it spread out around the Sand Dollar, returning to the sea. Rain flogged the restaurant, and beyond the swinging sign a set of running lights flashed offshore as a boat searched for any safe harbor before nightfall.

"Now I get it," she said. "You finally decided to take my advice and go home."

"Not yet," he said.

"You could have let me drive you . . ."

"Wait here."

"Oh, sure . . . !"

He grappled with the door handle. It wouldn't work properly so he had to reach outside to get it open. The door groaned as it swung out on mangled hinges. Across the almost empty lot, the restaurant's entrance was lighted, indicating that it remained open for business despite the storm, if for no other reason than to serve the stranded residents.

"Then wait in there."

"While you do what?"

"I have to find out."

"Find out *what*?"

"If this is the place she was talking about."

"Ruthie didn't know what she was saying . . ."

"Maybe she did."

"A castle? A round house with—?"

"With glass and roses. In the mountains. At the beach. I know."

"It was a dream. Juniors are like that. They fantasize, and they can't differentiate between their dreams and what's real . . ."

"Then maybe we should have listened to their dreams." He got one leg out and lifted the other one with both hands, as though it

293

were made of wood. "There's a place like that here. It was built back in the thirties by a famous architect. He called it the Round-house."

Lissa popped out of the other side, opening an umbrella from the back seat.

"All right," she said, "let's take a look."

"*I'll* take a look."

"You can't even walk!"

"I'm okay." He locked his knees and balanced first on one foot and then the other for her benefit. "See?"

"Jack, we should call the police."

"And tell them what? I'll check it out first. If I'm right . . ."

"Where is this place?"

"Up there. I'll take a look, and check it out, and come back."

"Promise?"

"Promise."

"Well, at least get out of the rain." She came to him with the umbrella, held it over his head, folded his fingers around the handle. She pushed his wet hair off his forehead. Was she going to ask him if he had milk money and clean underwear? "I'll watch you from here. If you don't come right back . . ."

"From there." He turned her around toward the Sand Dollar.

"All right, from there. If you're not . . ."

"You can't wait in the car. You'll drown."

"I know. I need a plastic sheet to put over the window. If you're not . . ."

"They might have one inside. Ask Jesus."

"Who?"

"He's the cook."

"Oh. Well, if you're not back in five minutes . . ."

"Twenty."

"Ten."

"Fifteen."

"Okay, fifteen—max. If you don't . . ."

"I'll be back, or I'll give you a signal. Then you can call the police. All right?"

"Where?"

He turned her shoulders to the rise behind the parking lot, back in the direction of the gatehouse, next to the gravel road they had come down.

"Look between the trees."

"*That?* How will you—?"

"There are steps. I know my way around here. You don't."

"Well . . ."

"The phone's by the cigarette machine."

"Between the restrooms. I know."

295

"Right." He squeezed out the back of her hair with one hand and laid it over her shoulders, arranging it in a fantail, the shape of a scallop shell. It was darker wet, with chestnut streaks, and incredibly fine in texture, baby's hair, really. It needed to be toweled dry. "Now get going. Here. Take this." He attempted to hand her the umbrella.

She broke away and ran to the sign and the awning. "You take it," she shouted.

He waved and turned away.

"Jack?"

"Yeah?"

"Is *he* in there?"

"Who?"

"Chris!"

"I'm going to find out."

"I'll be watching!"

"You do that."

Crossing the lot, he passed his own old car and three others. Each was locked tight against the storm, windows closed, rain beading on the tops. One was the skipper's; another, a VW bus with Bondo and primer around the wheel well, belonged to the bass player in the bar band; the third was familiar, too. He tried to place it. An old 2002, one of the last of the good ones, the kind you could pick up used for not much money a

few years ago, before the yuppies discovered
BMWs. It had a moonroof, an after-market
antenna . . .

Just like Lee's.

She had bought it after they were married,
with money she socked away from her new
job at the law office. Originally gray, she had
it painted royal blue, her favorite color . . .
Here, the gouges on the door, you could see
dull gray underneath.

It was Lee's.

What was she doing in Eden Cove? She'd
never been here before. Had she come to see
him? After all, she had gone to the hospital . . .

She'd be at the cabin, looking for him, or
Will. If she could figure out where it was.
Somebody would give her directions, down
the path, past the rich houses. He wouldn't
run into her. That was the opposite way from
where he was going.

He started up the high path, away from the
beach. Below him, he heard Lissa call out
from the restaurant porch:

"Remember . . . I'm watching you . . . !"

297

The air was filled with rain and the sound of wings, and the rusty skirl of a traffic light swinging from its cable, sirens, wet tires spinning through a flooded intersection, wild dogs barking somewhere far away, and the falling rain and the wings beating like blades, hovering, driving the water down in a circle.

The ground was rough and tarry. The rain poured into a fast-running river, echoing, blotting out the swishing tires and slapping feet, the sirens and the dogs, as if her ear were pressed to the opening of a seashell.

Leanne opened her eyes.

In front of her, within arm's reach, water coursed toward a storm drain, dislodging candy wrappers, bags, bottle caps, beer cans, newspapers, magazine pages, last week's *TV Guide*, all swept into the rectangular black slot at the curb, the launching point for a waterfall that would end underground. Raindrops as large as hailstones struck the pavement around her like machinegun fire, outlining her body on the asphalt. More water ran past her cheek, carrying a rainbow on its black surface. Her eyes smarted from the sting of oil. She shut them and raised herself on her elbows.

Two teenage boys saw her.

"Help me . . ." she said.

"Watch out for the bag lady!" one of them said, and they ran on, their white tennis shoes sending spray into her face.

She felt arms encircling her from behind and lifting her to her knees.

"Thank you. I don't know what happened. I . . ."

Rough hands shucked the coat from her shoulders, dragging it off.

"No, please . . ."

Her coat was gone, taken by a man with one shoe whose bare toes wriggled obscenely as he splashed away.

An ambulance passed.

She made it to her feet and grasped after it, clinging to a sign.

"Stop . . . !"

It sped on.

Beyond the east end of Main, roofs undulated under the helicopter's spotlight as metal blades sliced the rain. The copter banked and headed on to a convergence of ambulances and police cars at the base of the foothills.

Someone touched her hair.

She turned to see a child tugging at her curls with stubby, spoon-shaped fingers. She

realized that it wasn't a child but a man with
a short, round spider's body.

"You got a nice mane there, lady. Do you
braid it?"

Another hand came down and broke the
grip.

It was a bum with a big, pockmarked nose
and yellow in his eyes where they should
have been white.

"Leave her alone, Danny." He had the
breath of a fire-eater.

"Sez who?"

"The lady don't like to be handled."

She pushed away and moved forward into
the street.

The big man followed her.

"Some action, huh?"

"What is it? What's happened?"

"The bodies come down."

She saw vehicles at the start of the access
road, shapes moving on the hillside, some of
them hyaline-pale.

"One in the Fishers' backyard. Then one
come into Foothill Elementary. Then they all
washed down. From up on Old Oak."

He pointed at the access road.

The copter steadied its light as someone
tied something small and very white to a
rope. Then the rope was raised.

Now heavy, booted feet came up behind her. The drunken man saw who it was and backed away.

"Who's she?" he said, jerking his head at Leanne. Then, "All right, Eleanor, I'm goin' . . ."

A big woman shooed him away. He staggered off after the short, round man.

It was the woman with the shopping cart, from this afternoon.

She unbuttoned her coat, a quilted down jacket, stripped it off and wrapped it around Leanne's shoulders.

"You don't have to do that," said Leanne.

But she held up a hand, meaning *It's all right*. She had on several sweaters underneath.

"Thank you. Very much."

Touched by the woman's kindness, Leanne cried for a moment, then regained control. The woman's eyes, so inconsolable a few hours ago, were no less so now, but the pain and sadness there was now too much to bear, as if she stood on a gallows waiting for the trap to open and the earth to swallow her, as if it already had, many times over. Leanne shook her head to clear it, spraying diamonds of water from the ends of her hair.

A bullhorn rasped in the distance, directing traffic at the access road, as more sirens passed, every ambulance and police car from miles around, even the town's only fire truck.

The two women watched together. Leanne tried to remember how she came to be here. What had happened to her car? She needed to find a telephone, to call Steven. He'd know what to do. She felt an arm go round her shoulders. She began to get something from the other woman, no sounds, only pictures of a boy, a house, a man. As he turned to her, such a huge man and yet swift as a reptile, the lights and the pictures blurred and other pictures took their place, and she stiffened, shot through with the greatest fear she had ever known, a fear that had no bottom. She was back in the car, with him.

Bird-of-paradise plants bobbed under the raindrops and cocked their heads toward rambling roses. The rosebushes formed an arch, obliterating the latticework frame over which they had been trained to grow.

Bird plants, he thought. That was what the

little girl, Ruthie, had said. And roses. And glass . . .

There was the glass, all right, beyond the arbor, tall groups of panes stacked like a ladder up the front of the house and nearly touching the sky, holding reflections of the storm, the gray clouds and the lightning over the water.

Ruthie was right, he was sure of it.

The house was an avant-garde artist's dream. It had been built against the top of the cliff that was the edge of the coast highway, with massive trees behind to camouflage it from passing traffic. It was not visible from the lower levels of the Cove because of the tiered landscaping, except for a rare flash of silver or red if you happened to be looking that way when the sun set. He had asked Will about this.

That's the Old Man's, Will said. *The first house built here. Supposed to be a copy of a Gaudi.*

What's it like?

I wouldn't know. Nobody ever goes up there. The Old Man likes his privacy . . .

Now, as Martin came out of the tunnel of roses, he saw the high windows set into the sloping wood-and-plaster front, the extravagant molded detail work. It was a great

303

house in a distinctively eclectic sense, with none of the space-and-functionalism of Gropius and Wright but rather a feeling of organicism gone wild, with asymmetrical arches around a madly nonlinear façade, like a squashed gothic tower seen through the ergot-deranged eyes of a Bosch or Brueghel. There were balconies, turrets, a chimney squeezed out of a pastry tube. Ruthie knew a castle when she saw one. *In the mountains, at the beach.* Or at least the highest cliff that was anywhere near the water.

There were no stone steps. He hadn't thought so, had only said there were to get Lissa to stay down below where it was safe. A mossy path running with mud led in a maddeningly roundabout way to a tall door set back on a porch made of mortared cobblestones.

He swung one leg up, then the other, and prepared to knock.

As he left the path, riotous colors lanced through the climbing shrubbery, beaming down into his retinas. Martin shielded his forehead. Rain dropped into his eyelashes; he wiped it away, and located the source of the beam. It was a reflection from one of the Jacob's ladder windows on the second storey, where rays of colored light now streamed out through the glass, throwing moving pictures on the rain and mist. He couldn't make out what the pictures were, only spreading bands of apricot and cerise and vermilion, robin's-egg blue and blond-gold and an intense pink-white, the color of liquid flesh.

He looked again at the door, and saw that it was not black. It was already open, the interior of the house in deep shadow.

Leanne and Eleanor walked the length of Main with the storm at their backs. The rain and wind bent trees, splattered windows and roofs, blew into chimneys, whistling a warning. Leanne realized that the high notes were not really a whistling but cries, as women and men left their houses and walked, then jogged, then began running down Rosewood and Spruce, drawn to the hillside and the lights and vehicles already there. They ran by, calling the names of children who had not yet come home, sons and daughters they were afraid might never come home now.

"Jason . . ."

"Michael . . ."

"Jennifer . . ."

"Erica . . ."

"Amy, *where are you* . . . ?"

The canned voice of a newsman came from TV sets in every house. Cars from the other side of town began to pile up along the central artery leading to the fork. As she neared the access road Leanne saw a mudslide in progress farther up, the mottled outer layer shrugged off as the dirt underneath tried to hold to the hill, unearthing clumps on various levels that might have been pale subterranean larvae or marble headstones seen from a distance. The copter pointed its beacon, hovering like a bubble-headed dragonfly, while below policemen and firemen and paramedics received piece after piece of this strange bounty into their arms, zipped it into bags and loaded it into the trucks. Seventeen, someone said as Leanne got there, Jesus God how many more? It's the old riverbed, someone else said, it used to run from up there to the ocean, and that was right because the rills and rivulets that sluiced over the top seemed to be merging into a single strong and unified spout as it came down. There'll be more from up top, just you watch! It's that child-killer! They said they got him but they never did, and now look! Will you look, sweet Jesus, the rain's come and washed the rest of them out for everybody to see!

Eleanor strode past the police line to the ambulances, pointing her chin over the bodies to align her face over each child's, twenty-one of them now and still counting, but none fit the pattern she was looking for.

"Where's the Chief?" said Leanne.

No one listened to her. They were busy counting. Some of them got sick and had to stop.

"Chief Pennington," she repeated, "where is he?"

A young officer said with cracking voice, "He stayed up top, ma'am."

She remembered her vision of the Chief, and suddenly understood what it meant.

"You've got to go up there and stop him!" she said to the officer.

"Chief knows what he's doing. Excuse me, ma'am, would you stand aside?"

As he left the rain outside, he heard children laughing.

The house was musty and dark; no one had

307

bothered to turn on the lights. Martin put out a hand to steady himself, and felt his fingers slip into an alcove in the plaster. Something cold was there. His irises opened wide enough to see that it was a brass statue cast in the shape of a planet circled by rings. He bent close to it, catching the last light of day in the engraved lettering at the base.

SATURN AWARD FOR LIFETIME ACHIEVEMENT, read the inscription. PRESENTED TO ROY MILLER WISHMAN/ACADEMY OF SCIENCE FICTION, FANTASY AND HORROR FILMS.

So that was who the Old Man was.

He thought the director had died years ago, after a long and profitable career in exploitation films. How many had Martin seen as a teenager? The titles came back to him, as they had appeared on the drive-in screens of his home town: *The Hydra, Make My Blood Run Cold, Teeth, The Heart-Eaters* . . . They had seemed like truly great movies to him then, and had probably influenced the predilection for the horrific and sensational in his own work. The very nature of that work was what had prevented Martin from returning to it after the disastrous loss in his own life. Horror was no longer a delicious entertainment, might never be again now that he knew what real death looked like. It was too close to the knuckle.

The foyer opened to the left on a broad living room. Through the windows he saw raindrops coming down like hurled dimes. To the right, a stairway connected with the second floor.

That was where the laughter came from.

Martin grasped the balustrade. It was polished wood, but when he closed his fingers around it he thought there was a large splinter or exposed nail. It was his hand, where he had cut it on the hurricane fence. He took hold again, set one foot on the bottom step and started up.

The carpeting on the stairway felt soft underfoot. He took another step and it squished. How had the rain come this far in? And there was a dank moistness in the air. Martin thought of wet wool.

The laughter grew as the stairs took him higher. Definitely children. Giggling. The colors came again, spilling down from above, glancing off the framed posters for Wishman's later productions, a series of pretentious independent films in the 70's: *Mashed, The Corpse and Mrs. Miller, Necropolis, Deadeye, California Gothic, Quinterror, A Funeral*. They had effectively ended his ca-

reer, and he returned to Europe to die, or so
Martin had read. Instead Wishman had retired here, but perhaps not to die. . . . The
colors struck Martin like the rays from a
prism, the pure, natural hues contained in
white sunlight. The giggling was louder still,
along with another sound, a high, faintly
pulsing metallic screech that made the fill-
ings in his teeth hurt.

The bedroom upstairs was long, with a low
ceiling. It was arranged to double as a projection room, with perhaps a dozen beanbag
chairs clumped together in loose rows between the bed and the lenticular screen at
one end. An overhead video projector threw
an image that bled off onto the glass panes of
the irregular windows.

Martin's eyes followed the three-color
beam, and saw that the image was a scene
from one of Wishman's earliest, cruelest
films, *Somebody's Looking at You, Kid*, where
the nubile young actress is pursued by a
killer in a stocking mask. Or so it appeared
at first glance. The videotape copy seemed to
be overlaid with entirely different footage.
The effect was a trompe l'oeil of shadow and
substance, as if seen through a lace curtain.
He shifted his attention between figure and
ground, focusing on the superimposition.

The second film was a home movie of children at play, out of doors, and it was this soundtrack, the music of their laughter, that he heard.

How was it possible to show two tapes at once?

Another, single beam cut through the air several feet below it, from a film projector on the opposite side of the room. Its metal reels scraped with each revolution.

"Mr. Wishman," Martin said.

As he stepped forward, the beam from the sixteen-millimeter projector blinded him. He spread his fingers in front of his face and moved aside. Behind him, delighted children squealed from a loudspeaker.

Was anyone in the room?

A piercing scream sounded at his back.

He turned to the screen, as the young actress's silent stalking ended. The killer in the featureless mask leaned over her and took her life with a swift, sure stroke of his blade, while on the competing soundtrack children giggled and cavorted over a rock in a green garden. Then the metallic squeaking ceased abruptly, and so did the murder scene, as the reel stopped. The frame froze and burned through to white, leaving the screen to the videotaped children.

Martin saw them clearly now. They were pink and naked, little boys and girls no more than three or four years old. The rock they were playing on popped into three dimensions. It was not a rock but a bald head. Below the screen, a fat man sat on one of the clumped beanbag chairs, the top of his skull barely in the path of the video picture. His eyes were open, as was his mouth, which seemed unusually large. A pool spread out around the beanbag. The children laughed.

There was a sizzle, and the walls of the room became orange.

Martin turned back.

A flame burned in the corner, as a hand lit a cigar with a wooden match. In the flame, Martin could not see a face but only red streaks like the markings of a tiger mask.

He remembered the striking of another match, behind the screen at the drive-in theater.

"We've met before," Martin said.

The end of the cigar ignited.

"Is that Wishman over there?" asked Martin.

The match went out. The cigar arced like a meteor as the videotape on the screen across the room brightened to a sunnier pink. This new light showed Martin a man in a long coat, sitting back on a round bed. Next to the bed was a table that supported a Bell & Howell film projector and a humidor.

"I don't care what's happened here," said Martin. "All I want is the boy."

He made a clumsy step toward the bed.

"For the love of God, give him to me. He doesn't mean anything to you."

The next thing Martin heard was not thunder but a rumbling laugh.

Lissa didn't have a watch, but she was sure she had waited long enough.

The storm stood over the coast on tall legs blacker than the night. The sea tossed and whipped with whitecaps and the sign over her head creaked like a guillotine. The trees up the hill from the lot rustled and swayed, but Jack did not reappear. She pulled back the door to the restaurant and went inside.

Several regulars were at the bar. An old-timer with a beret shook knotty fingers at a woman in a clear plastic rain bonnet. A fisherman with tattoos drank Irish coffee and squinted over an unfiltered cigarette. The bartender waved at Lissa. She pointed to the hallway, where the restrooms were.

The walls were lined with relics: an antique lantern, a ship's wheel, a cleated coil of hempen rope, water-stained photographs of a bald man with a gaffed marlin, an albacore and a shark, next to a mounted swordfish with an iridescent dorsal fin rising from its back. She lifted the heavy, cold telephone receiver to her cheek.

She had no coins.

She left it dangling and started back along the hall. Then a thunderclap rocked the sky, and the lights went out.

She felt for the wall, waiting for the electricity to be restored. The rope might have been a scarred wrist, the swordfish fin a spiny batwing. The thunder came again. This time it was footsteps on the boards of the hall.

Something touched her between the shoulder blades.

"Need a hand?" said a man's voice.

She stopped breathing.

"I saw you come in . . ."

"Who's there?"

"Only me. Jesus."

Why didn't that make her feel any better?

"Can you fix the lights?"

314

"Give it a minute. Then I'll check the circuit breaker. If that doesn't do it, it's the whole Cove."

"How long?"

"Hard to tell. The storm could have knocked out a power line."

"I have to make a call."

"Where to?"

"The police."

"They can't do anything."

"No, it's not about that. It's an emergency."

"Go ahead. The phone company's got its own power."

Was that true?

"There's another problem. I don't have any change."

"Take some of mine, Miss Shelby."

She heard coins jingling, felt a new quarter with sharp ridges slide on her wrist, then into her hand. He had called her by name. She couldn't recall ever seeing the cook, if that was really who he was.

"Thanks . . . Do I know you?"

"Just call me the Friendly Stranger."

She found the phone. Before she could get the coin into the slot, it slipped from her fingers.

Shit!

"Did you hear where it fell?" she said. "I can't—"

The lights came on.

There was no one else in the hall.

She saw the quarter on the floor and stooped to retrieve it as a siren screamed into the parking lot.

She left the hall and pushed outside.

A County Sheriff's car screeched down past the gatehouse and braked, fishtailing on the flooded blacktop. Two uniformed officers jumped out.

"Here!" she cried.

They ran for the restaurant. One of them unsnapped his holster on the way. It was a Deputy from last night, at the bus site.

"How did you know?"

"Know what, ma'am?"

"I was calling . . . He's in there. The house behind the trees."

"And you are . . . ?"

"She's the social worker," said the other Deputy, older but not by much. "He's where?"

"This is Shelby?"

"Yes, I am. Listen, there's no time. Go up the steps . . ."

"Is that where he is?"

"I think so. The boy may be, too. I haven't

316

seen anybody come out, unless there's another way."

"What boy?"

"The little boy you're supposed to be looking for!"

"Call for backup," the older Deputy said. "Get Gloria to patch you through to Pritchard. Tell him we've got Wishman on a possible kidnapping with intent."

"Who's Wishman?" she said.

The younger Deputy got a suspicious look in his eyes. "Who are *you* talking about, ma'am?"

"Jack—Mr. Martin. He went in twenty minutes ago, and he hasn't come back."

"He knows Wishman?"

"No, he doesn't know him! He wanted to find out if that's where the boy is!"

"How did he know where to look?"

"He lives here, doesn't he?" said the other Deputy. "Him and his roommate. Pennington was right about something. They both knew, all along."

"Look," she said, "I don't know what you're talking about, but Jack hasn't done anything wrong. He's trying to *help*, don't you get that? He drew you the picture, didn't he? He found the first body, and he reported it . . ."

317

"It wasn't the first," said the young Deputy.

She was ready to burst. "Why are you standing here? I'm telling you, something's wrong in there!"

The people from the bar had come out to watch.

"Everybody inside," said the young Deputy. "We'll want to take your statements." Then he nodded at his partner, and they ran for their car.

Lissa followed.

"You too, ma'am. Stay back."

"Be careful with that," she said. One of them was unlocking the shotgun from the dashboard while the other phoned in. "Jack's wearing a tweed coat . . ."

The Deputy hesitated with his hand on the shotgun, and left it where it was for the moment.

"We'll wait for backup," he said.

"*Wait?*" She couldn't believe it. "You can't wait! He could be in trouble!"

She tried to see the house. She did not know where to look in the darkness. For an instant she thought she saw a colorful Japanese lantern floating in the air between the trees, but that couldn't be.

"Where is he?"

"Not here," said the man on the bed. His voice was a startling mixture of hoarseness and resonance, both shallow and deep, a low-pitched whisper from what must have been a barrel chest under the coat.

"Then where?"

"Safe."

Martin came closer, following the white film projector light back to the lens. He moved aside, out of the beam, so that he could see who the man was.

"Why did you take him?"

"Wouldn't you?"

Martin kept moving. "I tried to help him. He was scared of something. I think you're it."

"Scared of his own father?"

Martin hadn't expected that. Christopher had lived next door to Will with a handicapped mother, a father who ran off . . .

"You worked for him, didn't you? For Wishman."

"Once. A long time ago."

"He made this tape?" And, thought Martin, others like it? How many?

"It was—his hobby."

"Why did you come back?"

"The boy needed me."

The man drew on Wishman's fine Cuban cigar, savoring it.

On the screen, children like precious elves or sprites played over the rock that was Wishman's head, sunning themselves, innocent of shame without their clothes, unaware of his eyes and the way he had seen them through the lens of his magnum opus, the film that would never be released, made only to satisfy himself and others like him, his own straight-to-video director's cut.

How could so many children have been lured here without Will or anyone else knowing about it? The tape could be old, several years at least, before Will had moved here and taken the job at the gate . . . but what about the rest of the Cove? Unless they were all in collusion, there had to be another way into Wishman's garden, a secret way, one that didn't involve the main road.

Martin looked around for a hidden door, a maid's entrance, perhaps, that would open directly to one of the many overgrown footpaths on the hillside behind the house. There had to be one, a path that led up to the highway. A private access.

"That's not why," said Martin. "You came back because of Wishman. To procure for him, for one more movie. And whatever you did with them, after."

"Idiot," the man said. "He didn't need me. He found another bag man. I stopped doing this years ago, after my son was born."

The statement, so perverse in its irony, was all that Martin could take. Something snapped inside him. He would take this man down no matter what the price.

It was necessary to lure him off the bed, away from the wall and the darkness, into the open.

The film projector, showing only white, went off as though the power had been cut. At the same time the videotape of the laughing children slowed down and shrank to a brown circle. One little girl tossed her hair and stared into the camera, her eyes and her smile fading along with the sound of her laughter, giggling lower and lower in volume, as if drowning.

Now Martin was alone with the man in the dark. He heard him exhale.

"Couldn't you take the blood and guts? So many kids . . . What happened, did you fall in love with one? Was it the girl on the beach? I'll bet she had a nice little ass. Just about the right fit for you."

Martin heard raspy breathing.

"I never touched them. I was only the bag man. When he started again, I came back to finish it."

Martin applauded slowly. "What took you so long?"

The cigar rose and fell. "You can go now. It doesn't concern you. It's over."

"Not until you tell me where the boy is."

Martin saw the cigar rise higher as the man got up from the bed, passing him in a neon streak, leaving an afterimage. The cigar stopped moving and dropped to the floor.

Click.

"Time to die, little man."

Now the power came back on, and the projector and the videotape machine started again. The sound of the laughter returned, rising from the depths. The little girl grinned shyly and covered her eyes. The man was now in front of the screen. He wasn't that tall; the low ceiling made him appear larger. The naked children played over his body. Outside, a siren screamed into the parking lot. Distracted, he turned to Wishman.

"Seen enough yet, Roy?" he said to the dead man.

He picked Wishman up with one hand by his cut throat and held him like a fish by the gills in front of the screen, the bodies of the children projected over both of them, moving lips and ragged teeth and wide, shocked eyes.

"Then they can have you."

With his other hand he impaled Wishman on his knife in the middle of the chest and lifted him off his feet, swung him against the screen, knocking it over, and threw him out the window. The glass panes shattered and the body sailed out to meet the rain and dropped, crashing through the rose arbor below.

Now the video projected directly into the rain, coloring each drop, the children blurring as they joined the fine mist, softening and weakening, drifting and floating away behind gauze, their faces too dim to recognize so that they might have been anyone's children, breaking up into grain and color, form and the absence of form, separating and merging with the night.

Martin grabbed the projector from the table and lunged across the room with it, charging the broken-out window, spotlighting the figure still standing there. The man turned, knife in hand. The white light intensified as it stopped down on his face, blinding him. Martin's legs didn't give out, they felt fine, so he kept moving. The power cord played out behind him, went taut and snapped out of the wall. The man slashed his knife at the spots in the air.

"Who are you?" he said.

"It doesn't matter," Martin said. "I know who you are." He raised the projector over his head and heaved it at the face, laying all his weight behind it.

The man went out over the sill, taking the machine with him, like a scuba diver with an anchor dropping backwards out of a boat.

Martin waited for the crash, then looked out over the grounds. He couldn't catch his breath. He didn't want to. He felt exhilarated. From this far up the other houses and cabins were not visible through the foliage, as if they did not even exist. Only the ocean itself, framed by the most perfect location in Eden Cove.

There was the crash of glass and the sound of trees breaking. Lissa knew it came from the house.

The two Deputies left her and crossed the lot. When they got to the edge they split up, entering the foliage from two sides.

There *were* colors in the sky. Unbelievable though it seemed, she saw pictures on the air, broken up by the rain. She could not tell what they were. Then a bright beacon went on in the high turret window, shining like a lighthouse. As it extinguished a moment later she was sure she saw the silhouette of a man losing his balance, starting to fall. Before her heart beat again she heard him hit the ground.

"Jack!"

The Deputies were out of sight beyond the trees.

She ran, slipped in the water, got up and kept running.

There was only a dirt path, now shiny with mud. She left it after a few feet, and fell into rosebushes full of thorns. She righted herself and pushed on.

For a split second lightning illuminated a garden in front of what looked like a gingerbread house. Under the arbor, a man was helping another man stand.

He had survived the fall.

"Jack, are you all right?"

She had to get to him. Thank God for the Deputies. Now if they would call for an ambulance . . .

"Is he . . . ?"

The way the taller man was standing, a black hulk against the white house, she knew it wasn't either of the Deputies. And the man he was holding wasn't Jack; she saw the outline of a cap, a nightstick hanging from the belt. He was still trying to get his pistol out of the holster as the knife blade glinted. The Deputy's head fell back too far. Then the tall man let go.

She fought her way back through the roses to the parking lot.

The tall man came out after her.

"Halt!"

Lissa ran to the patrol car before she looked back. The other Deputy, the younger one, was a few feet behind the tall man. He had his weapon out, aimed with both hands.

"I said *halt*!"

He fired a warning shot, like the rulebook said. That made the tall man stop, long enough to turn around. The Deputy fired another round. Lissa saw water and blood,

326

green under the sodium vapor lights, fly out the back of the man's coat.

The Deputy waited for the man to fall. When he didn't, the Deputy shouted, "Put your hands on your head!"

That didn't slow the tall man. He was on his way to a car that was parked in the lot, a BMW.

The Deputy ran up to him and laid the barrel of the .38 on his jawbone.

"Get down—on your belly! *Now!*"

The tall man clubbed the gun out of his hand, at the same time bringing the knife up. It went in under the chin, up to the hilt. When he drew it out, blood splattered down as if from the neck of an animal in a slaughterhouse.

Then he got into the BMW and turned the starter over. The battery wound down and quit immediately, the ignition clicking, clicking uselessly.

He got out of the BMW and headed for the police car.

Lissa squatted down beside the car and tried the door handle. It opened. She fell across the front seat, reaching for the shotgun on the dash. One of them had started to take it and then changed his mind. Had he finished unlocking it? She grabbed the stock and pulled.

It came free, dropping into the crook of her arm like a lead pipe. She raised it and rested the muzzle on the dash, and looked out through the windshield.

A man was coming.

The shotgun was too long for her to get her body behind it and aim. She sat up, braced her feet on the radio, wedged the stock against the seat beside her, lined up the barrel as best she could, and yanked on the trigger with both hands.

Click.

"Pump it!" the man yelled, closer now, and she saw that it was Jack. She had almost shot him. But if that was Jack, then where—? "Take off the safety!"

A tall, black shape rose up by the driver's window.

No time to scream, she thought, as time slowed to a crawl. It reminded her of her first traffic accident, when she was a teenager. The driver ahead of her stopped at a railroad crossing where there was no train. She hit the brakes but too late. They locked, her wheels burning rubber as she skidded toward the rear end, unable to make her car stop. It seemed to take a long time, several seconds at least, for the impact, and all the while she was sitting there thinking *This isn't happening!* but it was and there was nothing she could do but ride it out.

And now here she was in another front seat. Time was standing still again. Except that this time there was something she could do. She had a 12-gauge over-and-under in her hands.

She swung it around and kicked the steering wheel, pushing herself sideways across the seat so that her back was against the other door. He was opening the driver's side. She raised the shotgun onto her knees. He was reaching in, reaching to knock it aside. She worked the pump and let it slide. He had the knife up, pointing down. She hooked two fingers around the trigger. He stank, his breath coming fast, inside the car now. She closed her eyes and pulled the trigger.

The sound split her head and the recoil kicked her hard in the stomach and knocked the wind out of her so that she could not get her next breath no matter how hard she tried. He flew out of the car and landed on his back six feet away. He couldn't breathe either, that was for sure, because there was a hole in his chest big enough to step in. She couldn't hear if he had made a sound, couldn't even hear what Jack was saying as he opened her door and put his arms around her to keep her from falling out. The first thing she did hear when she started to breathe again was clapping and cheering from the bar customers outside the restaurant, that and Jack's voice in her ear.

"It's finished," he was saying, over and over again. "It's finished . . ."

15.

A stocky man in a polyester suit climbed the hill. There were oak and birch on top and, farther on, giant redwoods that had deep roots in the decomposing rot and mulch of the forest. Unlike a man, they grew stronger because of it.

As he climbed, the sounds of helicopters and sirens and bullhorns grew weaker.

It was too late to watch where he stepped, because the rain had drenched and disrupted the ground everywhere, so that plants and insects and small burrowing animals alike had perished with water instead of air to breathe. He lifted his foot over a log, reflexively pulling up the crease in his trousers, and came down on a sinkhole in the earth.

The vines and branches that filled it rose

out of the mud and water at the weight of his step, reaching up to find something to hold onto or to drag down with them. He kicked, lost his footing, went to his hands and knees, saw the pale young tubers close like baby snakes around his wrists. As he twisted and flailed to free himself, he heard someone approaching in the darkness.

A strange calmness came over him. He ceased struggling. All around him the last raindrops dripped through the trees, growing fainter, like tiny footsteps going away.

As larger footsteps came closer.

Now that he was resigned, the undergrowth relaxed and released him. He crawled out of the hole and into a clearing that had once been a campsite. Past the stones of a firepit, there was a rocky cliff. He pulled himself up onto the largest of the rocks and looked out at the basin that formed the boundaries of Shadow Bay. The rain had washed the air clean and the eyes of the city were steady and unblinking, a thousand points of light spoiled only by the red blotches of police cars and ambulances.

Something was crossing the clearing, about to come up behind him, to the rocks where he sat at the edge with no place left to go.

He reached under his coat and took a .38 revolver out of his shoulder holster.

He looked at it as if it were a toy he had never seen before, turning it over in the first new moonlight that broke through the empty clouds. He dropped the cylinder, chucked out all the bullets but one, spun it and swung it closed.

Near his back, branches broke and vines snapped.

He put the gun to his head and grinned savagely.

"Too late," he said, "I win!" and squeezed the trigger.

The echo of the shot cracked like a whip against the hills.

Leanne's head jerked back at the sound.

No one looked up. It was only one more noise, a backfire, a slammed door. They were too busy to notice.

"It's too late," she whispered, as the dream left her.

Eleanor was opening layers of plastic to examine each face before the bags were taken away.

"Don't," Leanne told her. "What you're looking for isn't here."

"Could be," said Buffalo Bob. "Couldn't it?"

"No . . . I'm sure."

"How do you know, lady?"

"Her husband told me."

Eleanor stopped and looked at her, eyes burning.

"It's true. Your boy is alive."

The woman nodded once, without expression.

"She says thank you."

Eleanor started off, spotted the man with one shoe lurking in the crowd, hanging back, hiding in a new long coat. She held out a hand to him, palm up.

"Yes, ma'am," he said grudgingly. He took off the coat and handed it over.

Eleanor brought it to Leanne and put it on her shoulders.

"I didn't expect to see this again," Leanne said. "Here, take yours back."

Eleanor pursed her lips, the closest she could come to a smile. Then her expression hardened again. She gazed over the heads of the crowd.

"She wants to know where," said the

short, fat man. He tugged at Leanne's sleeve like a child at her apron strings.

"I don't know," she answered. "He had it blocked. In his mind."

"She don't understand," said Buffalo Bob.

"Neither do I," said Leanne. "But I saw the rest of it. You had a house, a life, money for the baby . . . Then what he was doing made him sick inside. He had to leave, don't you see? He was only—"

What? For Eleanor's sake she struggled to hold the memory of the pictures she had seen in the car, when she touched him.

"—Only burying. But even if he had gone to the Sheriff or tried to stop the one behind it, the law would have taken your child away. And he didn't want that. In his way, he loved you both too much. It was better for him to go away, no matter what that meant. You and the boy still had a chance, some kind of chance, that way. Without him."

There. It made little sense to her, would certainly not be any consideration in court, but it was the truth.

Eleanor looked up, as if at a tall, invisible figure before her, and made a cutting motion across her throat.

"She says, Then he dies now."

Leanne rested both hands on the woman's

shoulders. She saw sun on water and a home by the sea, a house that had become a trap, and diapers and bills and a man who was never there, a dream fading into ugliness and the battle for survival, which Leanne had known a little about, but only a little, she understood now. And she was not sure whether what she saw was part of a vision or merely a memory, pieces of old and broken dreams.

"He's gone," she said, and realized that she knew that now, too, as if the last knot in a string that had linked her to the man in the car had run out through her fingers. "It's already happened. It's better this way. Easier."

Leanne let her go.

A few older children hung around the police line. One by one parents took them away. There were four boys who went unclaimed for a long time, but eventually they, too, were found. The smallest of these, a wiry sixth-grader, dropped his attitude and turned on the little angel act when his mother showed up. A tough seaman with a scar slapped and cursed his wife as soon as she got into the station wagon. As they drove off, the boy in the back seat shot a poisonous, killing look at the man watching him in the rearview mirror, before his mother turned around to comfort him. Something about the look frightened Leanne.

"Who the hell is that?" said an ambulance driver.

He was standing on the tailgate, staring up at the hill and the access road winding down from it.

Someone came down the road carrying something. Lights went on, and she saw that it was the thin man from Box City, staggering under the weight on his back. He finally let it down into the arms of the paramedics.

Leanne shoved in next to them, and saw a muddy form. A flap of scalp settled back into place, sinking down over the missing part of a skull with crewcut hair.

"Jesus," said a Deputy, "that's the Chief! Who shot him?"

"Nobody," said the thin man. He handed over a .38 police special. "He dropped the gun. I saw the whole thing. It was an accident."

"Come with me . . ."

Leanne caught up with him after two Deputies left him by a squad car with all four doors open and the police radio squawking away.

"You carried him from up there?" she said.

337

"I couldn't leave him for the dogs."

"I thought you—your people would be gone by now."

"They went ahead. But I thought you might need some help down here."

"Did you know Chief Pennington?"

"Yeah, a little." His smile was gone. "He used to be my dad."

"Don't go anywhere," said a Deputy. "The Sheriff wants to talk to you."

"I'm truly sorry," she told him. She didn't know what else to say.

"It's really all right," he said. "I hardly knew him."

A pause.

"So. Will you be here awhile? In town?"

"Awhile. There are a lot of graves that need to be dug."

Another extended pause.

"How are the children at the camp? Are they all right?"

"Fair." He sat down in the car, shaky, and gave her his full attention for the moment, apparently relieved to make small talk. "How about you? Are you holding up?"

"Me? Sure."

His ponytail had come loose and his hair now hung over his shoulders, shiny-slick.

"You'll have to tell me about your Articles sometime."

"That? It's pretty simple . . . One, all debts are canceled. Two, no violence or physical force, against anyone. Three, you can do anything you want, as long as it doesn't hurt anyone else. That's it."

"I'll have to think about that."

"Let me know what you decide."

"I will. Listen," she said impulsively, "I—I have an extra room. It isn't much, but you can stay there anytime you need to. Like tonight. If you want to."

"I wonder what Barton would say?"

"The Professor?" She remembered the old man. "Why would he . . . ? Wait. I thought you said *he* was your father."

There was the smile, but weak. "I said he was my old man."

No, she thought.

"Oh," she said.

What could I have been thinking?

Hard steel grabbed her roughly by the elbow and forced her away from the car.

"There you are!"

It was Steven. His chest was huffing, pumped up like a bulldog's.

"Steven, if you don't mind . . ."

"I've been looking all over for you. They

339

found your car. It isn't damaged, I'm very glad to know. I've started the claim . . ."

"How are you, Steven?"

"I'm fine. I . . . are you okay?"

"I'm fine, too. Thanks for asking."

"Good. Now. Have they questioned you? Don't say anything. All you have to tell them is that it was registered to—"

"Steven, I'd like to be alone now. I'll call you. Later."

"But we have to talk about the . . ."

She left him.

The Chief's body passed by on a gurney.

I never got to tell him, she thought. I was that girl in the train station, in Kansas City. And I never even saw him. If I had, I wonder if I would have remembered?

Sheriff Pritchard came up to her. He was a junior-grade cowboy from Dust Bowl stock, with silver buckles and a Stetson hat.

"Mrs. Martin, we have your vehicle."

"That's nice."

"You can count yourself lucky. He committed three homicides an hour later, two of my best boys and a civilian, before we put him down."

"What civilian?"

"Name of Wishman."

"The killer." Not Jack. Then she caught

the last of the tall man's legacy of images, or at least her memory of them, before they drifted away and died with him. "Look in the house. You'll find pictures. The one who stole my car only did his dirty work for him."

"Who told you that?"

"He did. When I was in the car with him. He told me everything."

"I'll want to take your statement."

"Of course."

The clouds moved on, and she felt the last of the images moving on with them, lost to her, the minds from which they had come shut off now. Her thoughts would be manageable again now that they were gone. One, two, three . . . her consciousness invaded, as if she had been temporarily connected to them. What would it be like if more had come in, ten, a hundred, a thousand other people, if she and every other mind, every living thing were linked to each other, parts of one big shared mind?

It would be unbearable.

Jack would probably disagree. He might go for the mystical, may-the-force-be-with-you idea of it. Maybe it already was that way for him. Was that why he couldn't be more practical, because he was constantly dis-

341

tracted and overwhelmed by so many feelings he couldn't lock out?

No, she thought, I doubt it.

Where was Jack? He was one part of her, inside her, that hadn't shut down and gone completely away yet, though she had never had anything like one of those Vulcan mind-melds with him when they were married. I wonder if it would happen if I touched him now, his hand, say, just a handshake to say Good-bye, good luck, it's been nice knowing you . . . ? If she even had the ability, the capacity for it one more time.

There's only one way to find out, she thought.

Where *was* he?

She saw Eleanor and her three helpers watching from the sidelines.

"She wants to know where he is," said the short, fat one.

"So do I." Did they mean Jack? No, of course not. Then she remembered the boy.

"She wants to go to him now," said the big one with the nose and the breath.

"So she can take care of him," said the shoeless man.

"He's safe."

"You mean he got away?"

"I don't know." She took a look back

down Main, past the houses, the business section, the coastal homes, to the moon over a patch of sea. She didn't remember anything. The tall man had kept that knowledge locked away and hidden so far down inside that it had died with him.

"Tell her I wish I knew. We'll just have to keep looking."

Up on the hill, wild dogs started to howl.

Martin awoke under stars. He felt a sofa beneath him . . . Lissa's sofa, the edges of the cushions cold and hard. They weren't stars, they couldn't be. They were on the ceiling, one of those glitter-stucco cottage-cheese acoustic spray ceilings, in her apartment. Her condo. They were faint but comforting, in a way. Stars that never go away, no matter what happens.

He sat up and looked around her living room. A coffee table, a chair, a TV tube like a gray eyeball, taking it all in. Where was the tide? After living at the beach, the silence created a vacuum in his ears.

No, wait, there was a sound.

343

It came from across the room, behind a closed door.

A growling.

He got up and padded across the carpet, to her bedroom door. The growling was louder. He took hold of the doorknob, twisted it—

And recognized the sound.

It was snoring.

He smiled inwardly. Let her sleep till noon, he thought, even if tomorrow is a workday. He let the knob unwind slowly in his hand.

I should go to work, he thought. If it will come now. Something new, something clean and fresh, without reference to the past. All my paper and supplies are at the cabin . . .

Will's cabin.

Rest in peace, buddy.

I'll paint something for him, before the funeral, he thought. If he has a family, I'll give it to them. If he doesn't, I'll keep it for myself. Or give it to Lissa.

I could go to work for her, at the Hall, he thought. A lot that needs to be done there. I could teach art therapy, give lessons . . .

It might not pan out. The place was too much like a prison, windows that don't open, lock-down doors with chickenwire glass . . . I'd want to take the keys my first day there and go up and down the corridors, letting everyone out. And why not? It's going to be a lot safer around here now. There might not be any more need for facilities like McKenzie Hall.

Even if it was too late for Christopher. The boy would never be found, not alive. His body would turn up on the hillside in one of those shallow, freshly dug graves, or in an alley, or on a road somewhere, a sacrificial lamb. Martin had done all he could. It wasn't enough. But at least he knew that he had tried.

He crossed the room to the sliding glass door, let himself out onto the balcony.

A sea of stars spread over the salt flats, the old drive-in . . . There was the Milky Way, like a road to sail away on. To where?

I should talk to Lee, he thought. If I don't do it soon she'll be gone. We'll sell the house and she'll take her half and move someplace better, maybe all the way down to Malibu like she always wanted, if she can find a place to rent while she gets set up with a new job . . . She'll get one, a better one. She could do anything she wants to. She's smart. A lot smarter in most ways than I am.

And what will I do?

Go away for a while, from all the cars . . . Run mine into the sea. Get some distance.

Sitting by the pool at Quintas Papagayo, the sun on my nose, a fish taco in my hand, huaraches and a Mexican shirt, a liter of the best tequila in the world, and Noche Buena beer, then the Blow Hole, the Tivoli Nightclub, Hussong's, shrimps Veracruz, grilled corvina with lemon . . .

But that was another story. It was a dream. It would never happen. It wouldn't be the same now, without Will.

I could do some art down there, on my own, start with headstone rubbings in Guanajuato . . .

No. It would only turn bad there, too. The *policia* at the Point with semiautomatic rifles, the roots between the rocks, the anemones closing in, gourds and mushrooms rotting, the pastel gravestones, the pull of the riptide, the seagulls white as death's-heads, the dark ships at anchor . . .

You can run, he thought, but you can't hide.

He stood that way for an hour more, maybe two, under the Milky Way and the Pleiades so bright and yet so far away, trying to pick a direction.

The man knocked on the delivery door. He used his fist so the sound he made boomed off the bricks of the alley and shook the door like thunder. The boy put his fingers in his ears and waited for the pounding to end.

The door finally opened in a black line, and white fingers with shiny nails gripped the edge.

"Stop! Stop that or I'll . . ."

A pale man showed himself. When he saw who was knocking, his eyes went round and black behind his heavy glasses.

"You! I don't believe it . . ."

The tall man grabbed him by the necktie, dragging him into the alley like a dog on a leash.

At first Christopher thought he was hearing words in his mind again, but the pale man's eyes went even wider, so he must have heard it, too.

"Where?"

"I don't know what you mean."

One hand spread like a spider on the middle of the pale man's chest and pushed him

347

against the wall, holding him in place. The other hand brought the knife out.

"I don't, I swear! I haven't seen them in—"

Click.

The blade hesitated high in the air and angled down, poised to descend.

"Okay, okay!" *The pale man was blubbering, his face breaking out in red splotches.* "The group broke up after you left. Marion moved away, I don't know where, I swear to Christ. Jurgenson, too. The last I heard, he was in Pittsburgh . . ."

The blade nicked the air. The pale man's eyes followed it.

"The Old Man?"

"He's still at the Roundhouse, I guess. I never had anything to do with it, you know that . . . !"

The blade lowered and the hand crept off the pale man's chest.

"Let it be! It's over, I tell you!"

"It's NOT over. It's started again."

"What can you do? No one cares—if you do anything now, you're the one they'll want! You! They're not going to go after Roy. He owns everything, the real estate, the cops, the Mayor . . ."

"Does he own you?"

"Not on your life! I was only a fan! When I found out what was going on, I was outta there!"

The boy felt his feet leave the ground again. As he was thrust forward against the pale man's suit he smelled the acid reek of fear from the damp shirt, mingled with rancid butter.

"Keep the boy for me. For a little while."

"You can't be serious. How? I can't . . . !"

The blade lifted, stabbing the knot in the necktie, then flicked up, cutting through the cloth and coming to rest under the pale man's chin.

"Listen to my words, Lewis. This one is mine! If he is harmed, even one hair, I'll take your head. Do you understand?"

A hand on his back shoved the boy into an unlighted hallway.

I'm sorry.

No!

I can't take you there.

Don't leave me!

There is nowhere else, until it is finished.

But I don't want you to go! he thought, confused.

Wait for me . . .

349

Christopher fidgeted like a puppy dreaming of a run in sweet grass. He finally woke up when the hard thing at his back hurt so much that he couldn't sleep anymore.

He turned onto his other side, but he was not able to figure out what to do with his legs. The armrests were in the way. Then the sound of a scream jolted him, and he fell off the seat into the aisle.

The screaming ended and feet shuffled out on the other side of the curtained wall. For a moment he wanted very badly to go with them. Then he remembered that he must not.

He looked around in the green light from the EXIT sign, the door where he had come in from the alley. There was no other door except for the one in the back wall, where the projector was, and it was locked, too. He only wanted to get out long enough to go to the bathroom. There was still a half-full popcorn tub and lots of candy on the floor by the front row, where he had been sleeping, but the Monster Gulp Coke was empty.

A long time after the feet stopped shuffling and everything was quiet, he heard one more pair of feet come to the door behind the rows.

Somebody was trying to get in.

A key scraped the lock, and the door opened a few inches.

"Yoo-hoo, are you in there?" said a voice. "Everybody's gone home now . . ."

It was the scared man with the thick glasses and the shirt that smelled like butter. He walked down the aisle, rubbing his hands together.

"Where *are* you . . . ?"

The boy ran and hid behind the curtain on the wall.

"Come out, come out, wherever you are!"

The man went to the wall and started feeling along it, squeezing each fold.

"There you are . . . no? There! No . . . ?"

The shoes stopped in front of Christopher.

"There! Now I've got you!"

He wriggled out of the curtain and tried to run but the man had him.

"You can run, scream, shout, make all the noise you want, little piggy! It's very, very late, and nobody's home but us chickens!"

Christopher let the man lead him to a seat.

He won't hurt me, he thought. *If you touch him, Lewis, even one hair . . .*

"Is the little piggy hungry? How about a hot dog? Or are you thirsty?"

He didn't like the way the man's voice was changing.

"You'd damnwell better eat what I give you and learn to like it, because you're mine now, to do with as I please. Do you understand, little piggy?"

Wait.

All I have to do is wait . . .

"Be friendly, you little wretch! Nobody's coming back for you—he's dead. You're *mine* now."

It wasn't true. It couldn't be. He closed his eyes and searched for the sound of the voice in his head, of the one who was so much bigger and stronger than he was, and who he now understood was not the one at the top of the hill who had touched him but the other one, the one from his dreams, his protector and saviour. But the voice had gone away.

The manager's words became gentle again, dipped in honey.

"I've kept you safe, haven't I? I've fed you, kept number three locked so no one could disturb you, I've left you alone for all these hours . . . and now, is this the way you repay me?"

The boy ran to the curtains, the big ones in

front, and got behind, pressing against the screen, not moving, so small and so still that he was sure he couldn't be found this time.

The manager's voice hardened.

"I didn't bury the new ones as deep as your daddy used to," he shouted, "but I buried them just the same, remember that!"

The voice closed in on the other side of the curtain. How did he know where to look? The folds began to move, fluttering.

"Come to Papa now, little piggy . . . !"

He lifted up the curtain from the bottom as if raising the hem of a dress and caught Christopher in his arms.

He smelled of butter but his necktie was missing. Christopher remembered the knife point at the knot and smiled.

"Give Papa a kiss good-night, now. Then we'll play a game . . ."

Christopher went limp. He held his breath as the man's scratchy whiskers brushed his face. He shut his eyes as the hot tongue went into his mouth and down his throat. He only let one of his hands move slowly, so very slowly while the man squeezed him where it hurt.

Suddenly the man released him.

"What have you *done*? You've wet me!

Look at my *hand*! Why, I ought to kill you now, you little . . . !"

As the man loosened his grip, Christopher brought his penknife out of his pants pocket. He had the blade open in a flash, imagining that it went *click*! Then he moved it back and forth across the man's throat, making the first, then the second sideways lines for a game of tic-tac-toe.

The man stood up, turning around, clutching his neck, his mouth open, gurgling, trying to speak. He had lost his voice.

But Christopher had found his voice, his own true voice, at last.

"My turn!" he said, and laughed.